W9-BZQ-289

BOOKS BY
ALEXANDER McCALL SMITH

IN THE NO. 1 LADIES' DETECTIVE AGENCY SERIES

The No. 1 Ladies' Detective Agency
Tears of the Giraffe
Morality for Beautiful Girls
The Kalahari Typing School for Men
The Full Cupboard of Life
In the Company of Cheerful Ladies
Blue Shoes and Happiness
The Good Husband of Zebra Drive
The Miracle at Speedy Motors
Tea Time for the Traditionally Built
The Double Comfort Safari Club
The Saturday Big Tent Wedding Party

IN THE ISABEL DALHOUSIE SERIES

The Sunday Philosophy Club
Friends, Lovers, Chocolate
The Right Attitude to Rain
The Careful Use of Compliments
The Comforts of a Muddy Saturday
The Lost Art of Gratitude
The Charming Quirks of Others

IN THE PORTUGUESE IRREGULAR VERBS SERIES

Portuguese Irregular Verbs
The Finer Points of Sausage Dogs
At the Villa of Reduced Circumstances

IN THE 44 SCOTLAND STREET SERIES

44 Scotland Street
Espresso Tales
Love over Scotland
The World According to Bertie
The Unbearable Lightness of Scones

The Girl Who Married a Lion and Other Tales from Africa
La's Orchestra Saves the World
Corduroy Mansions

THE SATURDAY BIG TENT WEDDING PARTY

THE SATURDAY BIG TENT WEDDING PARTY

Alexander McCall Smith

Alfred A. Knopf Canada

PUBLISHED BY ALFRED A. KNOPF CANADA

 Published in 2011 by Alfred A. Knopf Canada, a division of Random House of Canada Limited, and simultaneously in the United States of America by Pantheon, a division of Random House Inc., New York. Distributed by Random House of Canada Limited, Toronto.

Knopf Canada and colophon are trademarks.

www.randomhouse.ca

Library and Archives Canada Cataloguing in Publication

McCall Smith, Alexander, 1948–
The Saturday big tent wedding party / Alexander McCall Smith.

(No. 1 Ladies' Detective Agency series)
Issued also in an electronic format.

ISBN 978-0-307-39826-0

I. Title. II. Series: McCall Smith, Alexander, 1948– . No. 1 Ladies' Detective Agency series.

PR6063.C326S37 2011 823'.914 C2010-904223-9

First Edition

Printed and bound in the United States of America

2 4 6 8 9 7 5 3 1

This book is for Professor Max Essex
of the Harvard AIDS Initiative,
in admiration of the work that he has done.

THE SATURDAY BIG TENT WEDDING PARTY

CHAPTER ONE

THE MEMORY OF LOST THINGS

MMA RAMOTSWE had by no means forgotten her late white van. It was true that she did not brood upon it, as some people dwell on things of the past, but it still came to mind from time to time, often at unexpected moments. Memories of that which we have lost are curious things—weeks, months, even years may pass without any recollection of them and then, quite suddenly, something will remind us of a lost friend, or of a favourite possession that has been mislaid or destroyed, and then we will think: *Yes, that is what I had and I have no longer*.

Her van had been her companion and friend for many years. Can a vehicle—a collection of mechanical bits and pieces, nuts and bolts and parts the names of which one has not the faintest idea of—can such a thing be a friend? Of course it can: physical objects can have personalities, at least in the eyes of their owners. To others, it may only be a van, but to the owner it may be the friend that has started loyally each morning—except sometimes; that has sat patiently during long hours of waiting outside the houses of suspected adulterers; that has carried one home in the late afternoon, tired after a day's work at the No. 1 Ladies' Detective Agency. And just like a person, a car or a van may have likes and dislikes. A good tar road is balm to man and machine and may produce a humming sound of satisfaction in both car and driver; an unpaved road, concealing behind each bend a deep pothole or tiny mountain range of corrugations, may provoke rattles and groans of protest from even the most tolerant of vehicles. For this reason, the owners of cars may be forgiven for thinking that under the metal there lurks something not all that different from a human soul.

Mma Ramotswe's van had served her well, and she loved it. Its life, though, had been a hard one. Not only had it been obliged to cope with dust, which, as anybody who lives in a dry country will know, can choke a vehicle to death, but its long-suffering suspension had been required to deal with persistent overloading, at least on the driver's side. That, of course, was the side on which Mma Ramotswe sat, and she was, by her own admission and description, a traditionally built person. Such a person can wear down even the toughest suspension, and this is exactly what happened in the case of the tiny white van, which permanently listed to starboard as a result.

Mma Ramotswe's husband, Mr. J.L.B. Matekoni, that excellent man, proprietor of Tlokweng Road Speedy Motors and widely regarded as the best mechanic in all Botswana, had done his best to address the problem, but had tired of having to change the van's shock absorbers from side to side so as to equalise the strain. Yet it went further than that. The engine itself had started to make a sinister sound, which grew in volume until eventually the big-end failed.

"I am just a mechanic, Mma Ramotswe," he had said to his wife. "A mechanic is a man who fixes cars and other vehicles. That is what a mechanic does."

Mma Ramotswe had listened politely, but her heart within her was a stone of fear. She knew that the fate of her van was at stake, and she would prefer not to know that. "I think I understand what a mechanic does, Rra," she said. "And you are a very good mechanic, quite capable of fixing a—"

She did not finish. The normally mild Mr. J.L.B. Matekoni had raised a finger. "A mechanic, Mma," he pronounced, "is different from a miracle-worker. A miracle-worker is a person who . . . works miracles. A mechanic cannot do that. And so when the time comes for a vehicle to die—and they are mortal, Mma, I can assure you—then he cannot wave a wand and make the car new again." He paused, looking at her with the air of a doctor imparting bad news. "And so . . ."

He had done his best for her, of course, and bought her a spanking new van, blue this time, with an array of buttons on the dashboard that she had not yet dared investigate, and with an engine so quiet and unobtrusive that it was sometimes possible to believe that it was not switched on at all and that it was gravity alone, or some other mysterious force, that was propelling the van down the road. She tried to appear grateful, but it was hard. It was true that the point of a vehicle was to get you from one place to another without incident, but that, she thought, was not the only consideration. If efficiency were the only value in this life, then we would be content to eat bland but nutritious food every day—and the same food at that. That would keep us alive, but it would make for very dull mealtimes. And the same was true of transport: there was all the world of difference between travelling along a highway in an air-conditioned bus, behind tinted glass, and making the same journey by a side-road, on a cart pulled by a team of mules, with the morning air fresh against your face and the branches of the acacia trees brushing past so close that you could reach out to touch the delicate green leaves. There was all that difference.

The tiny white van had gone to a scrap dealer, and that, she thought, was the end. But then she encountered a woman who told her that a nephew of hers had acquired the van, and towed it up to his place near the Tuli Block. He loved tinkering, she said, and he might be able to do something with the parts that he could strip from the body of the van. That was all Mma Ramotswe heard, and nothing more. It was a better fate, perhaps, than that of total destruction in the jaws of some metal-crushing predator, but still she hoped that the young man who had bought the van for scrap might exercise his mechanical skills and restore it. And that possibility she kept in her mind, tucked away among the other scraps of hope of the sort that we go through life with, not thinking about them very much but unwilling to let them fade away altogether.

Now, on this crisp Botswana day, at the tail end of a winter that, for all its cold mornings, was still drenched in clear and constant sun, Mma Ramotswe was reminded of her former van by something she saw on the road. She was driving past the Ministry of Water Affairs, her mind on a case that she had been working on for some time and was no nearer resolution than when she had started. She wondered whether she should not begin afresh, abandoning all the information she had obtained, and speaking to everybody again from scratch; possibly, she thought, it might be easier if . . . And then, out of the corner of her eye, she saw what seemed to be her tiny white van. It was not just that she saw a white van—they were common enough in a country where the most popular colour for a vehicle was white—it was the fact that the white vehicle she saw had the *air* of her van, a characteristic gait, so to speak, a way of moving.

Her first instinct was to stop, and this she did, pulling in to the side of the road, her wheels throwing up a cloud of dust and causing the vehicle behind her to swerve angrily. She waved an apology—that was not the sort of driving she condoned in others—before twisting round in her seat to look at the turning down which she had glimpsed the van making its way. She saw nothing, so she decided to reverse a few yards to get a better view. But no, the side-road was empty.

She frowned. Had she imagined it? She had read somewhere that those who mourn will sometimes see those they mourn—or will think they see them. But she was not really mourning her van, even if she regretted its passing; she was not the sort of woman who would allow something like that to get in the way of living. She shook her head, as if to clear it, and then, on impulse, made a sweeping U-turn, heading off on to the side-road down which she had seen the white van disappear.

A woman was sitting on a stone on the edge of the road, a small bundle of possessions on the ground beside her. Mma Ramotswe slowed down, and the woman looked at her enquiringly.

"I'm sorry, Mma," said Mma Ramotswe through her open window. "I haven't stopped to give you a ride to wherever it is you want to go."

"Ah," said the woman. "I hoped you had, Mma, but I don't mind. My son promised to come and collect me, and he will get round to it eventually."

"Sometimes men forget these things," said Mma Ramotswe. "They tell us that they are too busy to do the things we want them to do, but they have plenty of time for their own concerns."

The woman laughed. "Oh, that is right, my sister! I can hear them saying that in those voices that men have!"

Mma Ramotswe joined in the laughter. Then she asked, "Did a white van come down this way, Mma? Not a big one—a small one, same size as this one I'm in but much older—and white."

The woman frowned. "When, Mma? I have only been sitting here for half an hour."

"Oh, not that long ago," said Mma Ramotswe. "About two or three minutes ago. Maybe four."

The woman shook her head. "No, Mma. Nobody has been

down here for at least ten minutes, maybe more. And there have been no white vans—I would have seen one if there had been. I have been watching, you see."

"Are you sure, Mma?"

The woman nodded vigorously. "I am very sure, Mma. I see everything. I was in the police, you see. For three years, a long time ago, I was one of those police ladies. Then I fell off a truck and they said that I could not walk well enough to stay in. They are very foolish sometimes, and that is why the criminals sit there in those bars and tell one another stories of what the police have not done. They laugh at them and drink their beer. That is what is happening today, and God will certainly punish the politicians one day for letting this happen."

Mma Ramotswe smiled. "You are right, Mma. Those criminals need to be taught a lesson. But to go back to the van, are you absolutely sure, Mma?"

"I am one hundred per cent sure," said the woman. "If you made me stand up in the High Court in Lobatse and asked me whether I had seen a van, I would say certainly not and that is the truth."

Mma Ramotswe thanked her. "I hope that your son comes soon, Mma," she said.

"He will. When he has finished dancing with ladies or whatever he is doing, he will come."

MMA RAMOTSWE continued with her journey, completing the tasks she had been on her way to perform. She thought no more of the sighting of the van until she returned to the office a couple of hours later and mentioned the matter to Mma Makutsi.

"I saw something very strange today, Mma," she began as she settled herself at her desk.

"That is no surprise," said Mma Makutsi from the other side of the room. "There are some very strange things happening in Gaborone these days."

Mma Ramotswe would normally have agreed with this—there were very odd things happening—but she did not want Mma Makutsi to get launched on the subject of politics or the behaviour of teenagers, or any of the other subjects on which she harboured strong and sometimes unconventional views. So she went on to describe the sighting of the van and the curiously unsettling conversation she had had with the woman by the side of the road. "She was very sure that there had been no van, Mma, and I believed her. And yet I am just as sure that I saw it. I was not dreaming."

Mma Makutsi listened attentively. "So," she said. "You saw it, but she did not. What does that mean, Mma?"

Mma Ramotswe considered this for a moment. There was something on the issue in Clovis Andersen's book, she seemed to remember; *The Principles of Private Detection* had a great deal to recommend it in all departments, but it was particularly strong on the subject of evidence and the recollection of what people see. *When two or more people see something,* the great authority had written, *you would be astonished at how many different versions of events you will get! This is not because people are lying; it is more because we see things differently. One person sees one thing, and another sees something altogether different. Both believe that they are telling the truth.*

Mma Makutsi did not wait for Mma Ramotswe to answer her question. "It means that one of you saw something that the other did not."

Mma Ramotswe pondered this answer. It did not advance the matter very much, she thought.

"So the fact that one of you saw nothing," Mma Makutsi continued, "does not mean that there was nothing. She saw nothing because she did not notice anything. You saw something that she did not notice *because it was not there,* or it was not there in the way that you thought it was there."

"I'm not sure I follow you, Mma Makutsi . . ."

Mma Makutsi drew herself up behind her desk. "That van, Mma Ramotswe, was a ghost van. It was the spirit of a late van. That's what you must have seen."

Mma Ramotswe was not certain whether her assistant was being serious. Mma Makutsi could make peculiar remarks, but she had never before said anything quite as ridiculous as this. That was what made her feel that perhaps she was joking and that the proper reaction for her was to laugh. But if she laughed and her assistant was in fact being serious, then offence would be taken and this could be followed by a period of huffiness. So she confined her reaction to an innocent question: "Do vans have ghosts, Mma? Do you think that likely?"

"I don't see why not," said Mma Makutsi. "If people have ghosts, then why shouldn't other things have them? What makes us so special that only we can have ghosts? What makes us think that, Mma?"

"Well, I'm not so sure that there are ghosts of people anyway," said Mma Ramotswe. "If we go to heaven when we die, then who are these ghosts that people talk about? No, it doesn't seem likely to me."

Mma Makutsi frowned. "Ah, but who says that everybody goes to heaven?" she asked. "There are people who will not get anywhere near heaven. I can think of many . . ."

Mma Ramotswe's curiosity was too much for her. "Such as, Mma?"

Mma Makutsi showed no hesitation in replying. "Violet Sephotho," she said quickly. "There will be no place for her in heaven—

that is well known. So she will have to stay down here in Gaborone, walking around and not being seen by anybody because she will be a ghost." She paused, an expression of delight crossing her face. "And, Mma, she will be a ghost in high-heeled shoes! Can you imagine that, Mma? A ghost tottering around on those silly high heels that she wears. It is a very funny thought, Mma. Even those who saw such a ghost would not be frightened but would burst out laughing. Other ghosts would laugh, Mma—they would, although we wouldn't hear them, of course."

"Unless we were ghosts ourselves by that stage," interjected Mma Ramotswe. "Then we would hear them."

This warning made Mma Makutsi fall silent. It had been an appetising picture that she had been painting, and she slightly resented Mma Ramotswe's spoiling it like this. But her resentment did not persist, as it occurred to her that Mma Ramotswe, having possibly just seen a ghost herself—even if only a ghost van—might be in need of a restorative cup of red bush tea.

"I think it is time that I put the kettle on," she said. "All this talk of ghosts . . ."

Mma Ramotswe laughed. "There are no ghosts, Mma. No ghost people, no ghost vans. These things are just stories we make up to frighten ourselves."

Mma Makutsi, now standing beside the kettle, looked out of the window. Yes, she thought, one can say that sort of thing in broad daylight, under this wide and sunlit Botswana sky, but would one say the same thing with equal conviction at night, when one was out in the bush, perhaps, away from the streetlights of town, and surrounded by the sounds of the night—sounds that could not be easily explained away and could be anything, things known or unknown, things friendly or unfriendly, things that it was better not to think about? She shuddered. It was not a good idea to let one's mind dwell on these matters, and she was sure it was best to think about something quite different. And so she said to Mma Ramotswe, "Mma, I am worried about Charlie. I am very worried."

Mma Ramotswe looked up from her desk. "Charlie, Mma Makutsi? But we have always been worried about Charlie, right from the beginning." She smiled at her assistant. "I'm sure that even when he was a very small boy, this high, his mother was shaking her head and saying that she was worried about Charlie. And all those girls, I'm sure that they have been saying the same thing for years. It is what people say about him."

Mma Makutsi smiled too, but only weakly. "Yes, Mma," she said. "But this time it's different. I think now that we have to do something about him."

Mma Ramotswe sighed. Whatever it was, Mma Makutsi was probably right. But she was not sure that it was the responsibility of the No. 1 Ladies' Detective Agency to deal with Charlie's problems—whatever they were. Charlie was an apprentice of Tlokweng Road Speedy Motors, and it would have to be Mr. J.L.B. Matekoni who took action.

She looked across the room at her assistant, who was frowning with concentration as she poured the boiling water into the teapot. "Very well, Mma Makutsi," she said. "Tell me what the trouble is. What has our young friend been up to now?"

CHAPTER TWO

THE CHARLIE PROBLEM

THAT EVENING, Mma Ramotswe pondered what she had been told by Mma Makutsi. She thought about this while she prepared the evening meal, in an empty house, as Mr. J.L.B. Matekoni had taken Puso and Motholeli to choir practice in the school hall. Both children had good voices, although Puso was plagued by embarrassment when he sang, closing his eyes as a result.

"Puso," the choirmaster scolded him, "we do not close our eyes when we sing. We keep them open so that people who are listening know that we are not asleep. If you close your eyes, then maybe next you will start to close your mouth, and that is not good for singing, is it?"

In spite of this public upbraiding, Puso continued to close his eyes. The choirmaster learned to ignore the matter, though: the boy had a naturally good ear for music, and that was something that was worth cultivating in spite of other failings.

Mma Ramotswe went over Mma Makutsi's revelations about Charlie and made sure that she knew how best to relate them to Mr. J.L.B. Matekoni. It was a matter for adults to discuss among themselves, not one for the ears of children, so when the three of them eventually returned she fed the children first; that way, she and Mr. J.L.B. Matekoni would be able to talk freely.

"We shall have our dinner a bit later," she said to her husband. "If you are too hungry to wait, I can give you something. But it might be better not to eat until we can talk privately."

Mr. J.L.B. Matekoni nodded, and sniffed at the cooking smells drifting out from the kitchen. "It smells very good, Mma Ramotswe," he said. "So I shall wait."

"I have made—" she began, but he silenced her with a finger to his lips.

"It will be a surprise." He paused, before whispering, "What do we have to talk about that cannot be spoken of in front of the children? Is it one of your cases?"

She shook her head. "No, it is one of *your* cases, Rra."

He was puzzled. "I have no cases," he said. "You are the detective; I am only—"

She leaned forward. "Charlie," she whispered. "He is your responsibility, is he not?"

He looked grave. Ever since he had taken on Charlie as his apprentice—and that had been an inordinately long time ago—he had worried about the young man. At first his anxiety had been kept in check by the knowledge that apprenticeships do not last forever, but then the realisation slowly dawned on him that some apprenticeships appeared to disprove that rule. Charlie and Fanwell, his fellow apprentice, should have finished their training years earlier. Fanwell, at least, was now only a month or two short of completion, having at last passed the examinations of the Mechanical Apprenticeship Board and needing only a final period of assessment—a formality—before being registered as a fully qualified mechanic. Charlie, however, had failed his examinations time after time, mainly because he never bothered to prepare himself.

"You could pass very easily, you know," Mr. J.L.B. Matekoni

told him after the last unsuccessful attempt. "All it needs is a bit of study. You are not a stupid young man—you have a brain in that head of yours, and yet you will not use it. You are like a farmer who has good rich soil and plants no melons in it. That is what you are like."

"Mmm," said Charlie, licking his lips. "I like melons, Boss!"

"There you are," said Mr. J.L.B. Matekoni, with exasperation in his voice. "You are talking about melons when you should be talking about engines. That is exactly what I mean."

"But you are the one who started talking about melons," said Charlie. "I did not start it, Boss!"

It was extraordinarily frustrating, but it seemed that there was little that could be done. Mr. J.L.B. Matekoni was not only the finest mechanic in Botswana, he was also the kindest. And it was for this reason that he could not bring himself to dismiss the young man and give his place to another who was more willing to learn. Charlie would have to content himself with being an unqualified mechanical assistant—a sort of perpetual apprentice.

There were other reasons to worry, of course. There was Charlie's preoccupation with girls, and his constant talking about them. This distracted Fanwell, who was an altogether more serious young man, and it was also potentially bad for the image of the garage. On more than one occasion, Mr. J.L.B. Matekoni had been embarrassed in the presence of a client when the idle, girl-focused chatter of his apprentices had been quite audible. This had even happened once when a client who was a man of the cloth had been collecting his car and had heard Charlie talking about a girl. The two young men were under a truck and were probably unaware of the presence of the minister, but even so it had been a very awkward moment for their employer.

"Boy, oh boy," Charlie had said, "that one is very fast! She is fast all right!"

Mr. J.L.B. Matekoni had cleared his throat and done his best to spare the minister's blushes. "They are talking about a car," he explained hurriedly. "A very fast car. You know how young men are about speed."

He had raised his voice as he gave this explanation, in the hope that Charlie would realise they were not alone. But this had been to no avail.

"And she drinks too," Charlie continued. "I'm telling you, Fanwell, she likes her drink. Ow!"

"That is fuel consumption," said Mr. J.L.B. Matekoni to the minister. "Some cars these days have a very thirsty engine. It's because modern engines are so powerful. Unlike your car here, Reverend." And with that, he had given the side of the minister's car a loud tap, again in the hope of sending a message to the young men.

It made Mr. J.L.B. Matekoni feel hot at the back of the neck just to think about that moment—the minister had not been fooled—and he did not like to remember it. So when Mma Ramotswe told him that they needed to talk about Charlie, he sighed with a dread that seemed quite to take away any pleasure brought by the anticipation of dinner. A good meal is not nearly so attractive, he mused, if it is accompanied by thoughts of young men like Charlie.

SO, MMA RAMOTSWE," said Mr. J.L.B. Matekoni. "So you have made me a very good stew." He sniffed at the delicious steam rising up from his plate. "But you have also warned me that we have a Charlie problem. Tell me: Is it a big Charlie problem or a little one?"

Mma Ramotswe could not stop herself from smiling.

"Did I say something funny?" asked Mr. J.L.B. Matekoni. "You did say that—"

"Oh yes, Rra. I did say that we have to talk about Charlie. And it is a serious matter. It's just that the answer to your question is that this problem is both big and little."

Mr. J.L.B. Matekoni stared at her. Perhaps his wife had spent too long a time as a private detective and solver of mysteries; maybe too much time in that profession made one inherently enigmatic. He had seen that sort of thing before—cases where people had been so affected by their jobs as to change in their very nature. His cousin who had worked for the immigration authorities had become so suspicious that he began to suspect that just about everybody was in the country illegally. And then there was that butcher who had ended up not eating meat at all and would only eat potatoes and beans—that had been a very surprising development in a country as committed to cattle as was Botswana. Was something similar happening to Mma Ramotswe, he wondered?

"You'll have to explain, Mma Ramotswe," he said. "I am a simple mechanic; I am not a solver of puzzles and things like that."

Mma Ramotswe dipped her fork into her mashed pumpkin. "It is a big problem because it's serious," she said. "It is a small problem because it involves something small. A small person. In fact, it involves . . . a baby."

Mr. J.L.B. Matekoni closed his eyes. It did not matter if Mma Ramotswe said nothing more. He understood.

He opened his eyes again. Mma Ramotswe was looking at him, and she was no longer smiling. "Yes," she said. "You know what I'm going to say, don't you, Rra?"

"Charlie has a baby."

"Yes." And then she added, "Two. Twins. Two boys."

There was a silence.

"You had better tell me, Mma Ramotswe. I am strong. I have heard everything before. There can be no surprises when it comes to that young man."

"Listen to this, then," she said.

She retold the story she had heard from Mma Makutsi. It was related in a quiet, matter-of-fact way, without any of the short gasps of disapproval and tut-tuts with which Mma Makutsi had punctuated her narrative. But it was still enough to distract Mr. J.L.B. Matekoni from his stew, which became colder and colder on the plate.

Mma Makutsi had heard the story from an entirely unimpeachable source—the mother of the young woman who had given birth to Charlie's twins. She was related in a distant way to Phuti Radiphuti, and together with her husband ran a painting and decorating business in the west of the city. The business had prospered and now employed more than fifty painters; its name, Second Coat, could be seen on vans throughout the town, and they had several important contracts with large concerns, including diamond companies.

This couple, Mma Makutsi had gone on to explain, were called Leonard and Mercy Ramkhwane. They were hard-working and were thought to have deserved every bit of their success. They had only one child, Prudence, who was now in her early twenties. She had been at Gaborone Secondary School and had been a very well-known high-school athlete who had taken all the trophies for running. "It was a big pity that she did not run away from Charlie," Mma Makutsi had observed. "Many girls would do far better to run away from men, Mma."

The story continued. Charlie had met Prudence when Leonard brought a car into the garage for attention. On hearing this, Mr. J.L.B. Matekoni groaned. "I know that man," he said, putting a hand to his head. "I do not know him well, but I know him."

Mma Ramotswe lowered her eyes. "Well, he brought his daughter with him to the garage."

Mr. J.L.B. Matekoni groaned again. "So that means she met Charlie under my roof."

"No," said Mma Ramotswe. "The garage roof is not your roof. This is your roof here—in this house. There is a difference, Rra."

He shook his head. "It is my roof. I own it. When it leaks, I am the one who must fix it. That means it is my roof, and I am responsible for what happens under it."

She tried, with gentle persuasion, to convince him that he could not possibly be held responsible for Charlie's meeting Prudence, but his view was not to be changed. So she continued the tale, just as it had been told her by Mma Makutsi.

Charlie had somehow managed to make an arrangement with Prudence—under the very eyes of her father—to meet at a club that young people favoured. Good music, he had said; the latest thing. And what girl could resist such an invitation? Not Prudence, it seemed, and the inevitable happened. At first their relationship was kept secret from her parents; she still lived at home, but, at twenty, was largely independent. But then Charlie became the established boyfriend, and although not what Leonard and Mercy had had in mind for their daughter, he was treated with the courtesy and graciousness a couple like that would always accord to others.

"They are good people, you see," said Mma Ramotswe. "They follow the old Botswana ways. They are polite."

Mr. J.L.B. Matekoni nodded. Charlie did not follow the old Botswana ways. The old Botswana ways would never have approved of using a hammer to move a reluctant nut on an engine manifold. The old Botswana ways respected the *thread* of a bolt; the old Botswana ways understood the consequences of putting diesel in a petrol engine; the old Botswana ways . . . You could go on.

The relationship had been going on for a month or two when Prudence realised that she was pregnant. She told Charlie, and then she told her parents. Charlie left.

"Left her entirely?" asked Mr. J.L.B. Matekoni. "Altogether?"

It was Mma Ramotswe's turn to sigh. "No more calls on that phone of his, the silver one. No more going round to her parents' house. Nothing."

"They call that leaving somebody in the lurch," muttered Mr. J.L.B. Matekoni. "So what happened, Mma Ramotswe?"

"The girl calmed her father down. Apparently the old Botswana ways deserted him for a while, but he did not do anything. And that was that. Twins arrived. So Charlie is now the father of twins."

"He knows that?"

"Oh, he knows that all right. I'm sure she told him."

"And . . ."

Mma Ramotswe spread her hands in resignation. "And nothing. Charlie has done nothing." She sat back in her chair, indicating that this was the end of the story, or at least the end of what she knew of the story.

Mr. J.L.B. Matekoni looked down at his plate. He had touched very little of the stew she had made him—that delicious serving of Botswana beef—and now it was quite cold.

"I shall heat it up again for you," offered Mma Ramotswe.

He shook his head, reaching for his fork. "I do not mind, Mma. Your cooking is always so good that it does not matter whether it is hot or cold. Either way it is all that a man could ever desire. And that is the truth."

She smiled at him. This was how a man should be, she thought. And there was Charlie, working every day with this great man, this embodiment of all that the country stood for, and none of it, not one tiny bit, seemed to rub off on the young man.

She wondered whether to bring up the subject of what they

were to do now, or whether to move on. She decided on the latter. It was sometimes best, she believed, to let things sink in before you took a decision. So they would sleep on this disclosure and talk about it the following day, or even the day after that. Not that there was much to be said, as there was really only one thing to do in these circumstances. And that was to try to get Charlie to face up to his responsibilities.

It was easier said than done—Mma Ramotswe was well aware of that. Charlie would either deny that he was the father, or he would shrug his shoulders in that stubborn way of his and say that the twins were the young woman's affair. "Children are not men's business," he had said once. "It is women who must look after them, not men. These people who say that men must do that work too are talking nonsense, and they are all women anyway. Men have far more important work to do than that. Ha!"

Mma Makutsi had overheard this remark and had been so cross that her glasses misted over; that was always a bad sign, Mma Ramotswe knew. The recollection of this gave her an idea: they could ask Mma Makutsi to deal with the problem of speaking to Charlie. They would give her their full support, she thought, but the leader of the campaign—the general, so to speak—should be Grace Makutsi, recipient of the highest mark in history in the final examinations of the Botswana Secretarial College (ninety-seven per cent) and scourge of all those who would shift their feet, look the other way, or, for that matter, deny the existence of twins.

Yes, she was the one.

CHAPTER THREE

YOU ARE THE LADY TO HELP PEOPLE

SEATED AT THEIR RESPECTIVE DESKS, at a time when the morning air was still fresh and clear and the sky quite empty of clouds, Mma Ramotswe and Mma Makutsi surveyed what the day had in store for them. There were two appointments, one at ten o'clock and one not until well into the afternoon. The second appointment was straightforward enough—a discussion about a statement Mma Ramotswe was to make in a child custody case: simple, perhaps, but emotionally testing nonetheless. "You cannot divide a child's heart in two," she had observed to Mma Makutsi, "and yet that is what some people wish to do. A child has only one heart."

"And the rest of us?" Mma Makutsi had asked. "Do we not have one heart too?"

Mma Ramotswe nodded. "Yes, we have only one heart, but as you grow older, your heart grows bigger. A child loves only one or two things; we love so many things."

"Such as?"

Mma Ramotswe smiled. "Botswana. Rain. Cattle. Friends. Our

children. Our late relatives. The smell of woodsmoke in the morning. Red bush tea . . ."

That was the afternoon appointment; ten o'clock would be different. She knew nothing about the man who had telephoned and arranged to see her, nothing beyond his name and the fact that he lived outside town. He had not wanted to come into the office—a common concern for clients, who appeared to worry they might be seen entering the premises of the No. 1 Ladies' Detective Agency. Mma Ramotswe understood this, even if she sought to reassure them that nobody really paid much attention to those who crossed her doorstep. She wanted to believe that, and almost convinced herself, but she was not sure that it was entirely true. People noticed things in Botswana; they saw who went into which house and they speculated as to what took them there; they noticed who was driving which car and who was in the passenger seat. People saw these things, in much the same way as an expert tracker in the Kalahari will look at the ground and see, written in the sand, the history of all the animal comings and goings.

"I do not wish to come into your office, Mma," the caller had said. "I do not wish to offend you, but when you have a business like mine, you have to be careful. People might see."

"If that is what you wish, Rra, then that is not a problem for me. We can meet somewhere else. There is a café I know at Riverwalk. You know that place?"

There was a mumbling at the other end of the line, as if somebody was being consulted. Then the voice said, "I am a bit out of touch with town, Mma, but I can find out about it. I have friends who know Gaborone well. I can be there."

The caller had given his name, Botsalo Moeti, and had said that he would be coming into town from a place to the south of

Gaborone. "Not a village you will know, Mma, as it is very small. I need not give you its name."

"But that would be helpful, Rra. I might know it."

This was greeted with silence. "I do not think so, Mma. As I said, it is very small."

She had not pressed the issue, and the matter was left there. But after she had rung off and replaced the telephone handset in its cradle, she had looked across the room at Mma Makutsi and said, "That man is scared, Mma. I can tell it in his voice."

Mma Makutsi's eyes had widened behind her large round glasses. "There are many people who are frightened of something or other, Mma," she said. "Even here in Botswana there are people who are frightened."

They had looked at each other without saying anything. Each knew what the other meant; each knew that there were things that people preferred not to acknowledge, not to admit, lest the admission encourage that which needed no encouragement.

It was Mma Ramotswe who broke the silence. "I am not going to be frightened, Mma Makutsi."

Her assistant took off her glasses and polished them energetically with her handkerchief. "And I am not going to be frightened either, Mma. Even if . . ."

"Even if what, Mma?"

Mma Makutsi shook her head; she had said enough, she felt.

AT NINE-FIFTEEN, three-quarters of an hour before Mma Ramotswe was due to meet Mr. Botsalo Moeti, Mma Makutsi made tea. This was an occasion that was an established fixture in the timetable of the No. 1 Ladies' Detective Agency, but less observed in the daily programme of Tlokweng Road Speedy Motors, with whom Mma Ramotswe and Mma Makutsi shared premises. Mr.

J.L.B. Matekoni was happy to punctuate the day with tea, but only downed tools if the work in which he was engaged had reached a natural break. This meant that out of every five tea-breaks, he and his apprentices usually took only three, or sometimes just one or two.

"Everybody else has a regular tea-break, Boss," complained Charlie. "Go into a government office and what do you see? Everybody drinking tea. Same thing in the banks. More tea. Why not us?"

"Because we are not an ordinary business," sighed Mr. J.L.B. Matekoni. "Nor are we a government department. We are like a hospital—a hospital for cars. Hospitals do not suddenly say, 'We have had enough; we are going to stop curing people while we have a cup of tea.' They do not say that, Charlie."

The analogy with a hospital appealed to him, and he developed it in an attempt to get Charlie to understand the need to care about his work. "Yes, we are a hospital for cars, and you and I—what are we? We are surgeons, Charlie; that is what we are. And if you go into a hospital, do you see the surgeons using hammers on their patients? Spanners, not hammers: remember that."

The question was a pointed one. He had tried so often to stop Charlie's tendency to use a hammer on recalcitrant engine parts, but his efforts had met with little success.

"They don't use spanners either," said Charlie, winking at Fanwell.

Mr. J.L.B. Matekoni sighed. He sighed a great deal in his conversations with Charlie. "It is not something to laugh about."

Charlie adopted a serious expression. "I am not laughing, Boss, even if I'm thinking of a surgeon using a spanner on some poor man. Ow! Like this. Ow!"

"He would use an anaesthetic before he got out his spanner," said Fanwell. "We do not give anaesthetics to cars."

That morning the making of tea came at a time when the workshop was quiet, so both apprentices and Mr. J.L.B. Matekoni joined the two ladies in the agency office. Mr. J.L.B. Matekoni came in first, to be greeted politely by Mma Makutsi. Then came Fanwell, wiping his hands on a blue paper towel, and finally Charlie. As Charlie entered, Mma Makutsi glanced over at Mma Ramotswe. Nothing further had been said since their discussion the previous day, and Mma Ramotswe had not yet raised with her assistant the question of her tackling the young man; but nonetheless a meaningful look was exchanged. Mma Ramotswe hoped that Mma Makutsi would not launch into her own attack there and then: she could be impetuous, and might not judge her moment too well. Holding her assistant's eye, she mouthed the word "No."

Returning to her chair, Mma Makutsi took a sip of tea. "Well, Mr. J.L.B. Matekoni," she said brightly, "any well-known cars in trouble?"

Mr. J.L.B. Matekoni nursed his mug in cupped hands. "Nothing," he said. "We fixed Bishop Mwamba's car last week, and that tall government minister's car the week before that. This week it is just ordinary cars—no well-known ones."

"All cars are important, Boss," ventured Fanwell. "You said that yourself."

"Of course they are," said Mr. J.L.B. Matekoni. "We treat all cars the same."

Mma Makutsi was watching Charlie, who was leaning against a filing cabinet. Becoming aware of her scrutiny, the young man gave her a deliberately nonchalant stare.

"What about those vans?" she asked.

Mr. J.L.B. Matekoni frowned. "What vans?"

Mma Makutsi spoke slowly and deliberately. "The painters'

vans. The ones that belong to that nice man—what is his name?—Leonard something-or-other."

There was a sudden silence, at least in that small office; outside, the cicadas, indifferent to human drama, continued their screech. Charlie stood quite still, his mug of tea suspended in mid-air, unsipped.

Mma Makutsi continued regardless. "I thought you were hoping that he would bring all those vans in here. That would be very good business, wouldn't it?"

Mr. J.L.B. Matekoni looked anxiously in Mma Ramotswe's direction. "Yes," he muttered, "that would be good. But I'm sure that he has an arrangement in place for his vans. They do not seem to be breaking down—somebody must be looking after them."

"I thought he was a very nice man," continued Mma Makutsi. "But I don't know him, really." She paused. "Phuti does, though. He knows that whole family. The husband, the wife, the daughter—"

"Mma Makutsi," blurted out Mma Ramotswe, "look at the time! Here we are drinking tea, and I have to get ready to go to meet a client. We must get ourselves organised. Come on, everybody, drink up. Tea-time over. Right now. Over."

SHE WAS EARLY for her appointment and decided to spend a few minutes window-shopping at one of the clothes shops inside the rambling Riverwalk complex. She had no intention of buying anything—money was tight, with several clients being slow to pay their bills that month—but she felt that it never did any harm just to look. In fact, Mma Ramotswe found as much pleasure in looking as in an actual purchase; more perhaps, because looking involved no guilt, whereas purchasing often did.

This was something that Mr. J.L.B. Matekoni, in common with

most men, simply did not understand. "The whole point about shopping," he had remarked, "is that you go somewhere and you buy something you need. Then you take it home and use it. That is what shopping is about."

Mma Ramotswe had shaken her head. "No, Mr. J.L.B. Matekoni. You are right about many things, Rra, but you are not right about that. That is not what shopping is about."

He had been perplexed. "Then perhaps I'm missing something."

"Yes, you are."

"Tell me, then, Mma Ramotswe, what is shopping for? It seems that I have misunderstood the whole thing."

She smiled. There was much that men simply did not understand, but she had never been much concerned about this lack of understanding. Indeed, in her view it was one of the things that made men so appealing. There were men's things and then there were women's things. The list of which was not written in stone, and it was quite possible for a woman to enter the world of men—and the other way round—but she saw no point in denying that women liked to do certain things and men liked to do other things. Nor did she doubt that these preferences were one of the reasons why women liked men and men liked women. So it was perfectly possible that there were men who liked shopping, and who understood exactly what it was all about, but Mma Ramotswe had yet to meet such a man. Maybe they existed elsewhere—in France, perhaps—but they did not seem to be much in evidence in Botswana.

Of course, she knew that you had to be careful about this sort of thing. Like all women, she had suffered the put-downs of men, and there were still plenty of men who were prepared to say to women, *You cannot do this, you cannot do that, because you are just a woman*. She remembered many years ago, as a girl in the national school at Mochudi, hearing a teacher—a man—say to the class: "These are good jobs for boys, but not for girls; girls can do something else." She had smarted at the injustice. Why could women not do those jobs? You did not have to be strong, with bulging muscles, to be a pilot or an engineer, or a president, for that matter. Such men, she discovered, such men who put women down, were really rather weak themselves, building themselves up by belittling women. A truly strong man would never want that.

A truly strong man . . . Mr. J.L.B. Matekoni was one such, and so, too, had been her father, the late Obed Ramotswe, that great man, that good man, who had never suggested that there were any limits to what she could do with her life. He had been old-fashioned, it was true, but he had always said that women should stand on their own two feet and do what they wanted. And in many respects he had clearly been in advance of his time when he had remarked, as he often did, that the day when women took over important jobs from men would be the day that things got better. But not even Obed Ramotswe, her precious daddy, understood shopping as a woman understands it. He would not have wanted to linger, as Mma Ramotswe now did, before the window of a clothing shop and admire the tempting display within.

She gazed at the window. The proprietors of this shop had understood the situation very well: they sold clothing for both men and women, but in their window the women's clothes were tastefully displayed, adorning coquettishly posed mannequins or draped temptingly on small supports, whereas the men's clothing, distinctly less colourful, was simply placed on a low wooden table with the price tags showing. She saw that the women's clothing had no prices; that was as it should be, because if the price were to be displayed then that would spoil the fun of potential customers outside. They might be put off by realising that they could not afford this dress or that dress, whereas with no prices attached, they could dream of affording them all.

She noticed, too, that the mannequins modelling the dresses—those posturing moulded figures—were all waif-like and thin, as if the slightest wind might come and blow them away like so many leaves. Why were there not any traditionally built mannequins? Why were there not comfortable ladies in the window, ladies with whom those on the other side of the glass—not thin and hungry ladies, but ladies whose breakfast had clearly been generous enough to see them through the day—could identify? That was another thing that women had to be wary of, thought Mma Ramotswe; that was another way of putting women down—telling them that they should stop eating.

Her eye wandered to a small display of women's shoes in one corner of the window. One pair, in particular, caught her attention: cream-coloured, with high heels and two small buttons to fasten the straps. These shoes, she thought, would very much appeal to Mma Makutsi, and would be suitable for her wedding. There was talk of a date now, and she must be thinking about her bridal outfit. These shoes would go well with a white dress, but especially appealing to Mma Makutsi would be the buttons, each of which had a single mock diamond, winking even now in reflected light like little beacons. She would tell her about them; perhaps she would even suggest that they visit the shop together so that she could advise.

She glanced at her watch and dragged herself away from the window display. The café, which was round the corner, overlooking a parking lot, was a favourite of hers as it afforded a good view of one of the entrances to the shopping centre. If you sat there long enough, as Mma Ramotswe occasionally did, you might observe all

Botswana pass by, or at least a large part of it, and you would never fail to see at least one friend to whom you might give a wave.

As she approached the café, she realised that she had said nothing to her client as to how they might recognise one another. What if there were several men sitting at tables by themselves, as sometimes happened? Would she have to go up to each and say, "I am Mma Ramotswe"? This could be embarrassing, as the man would be obliged to give his own name and enquire after her health—if he had any manners at all—and then there would be an awkward silence. And Mma Ramotswe would then say, "And what is troubling you, Rra?" and he would reply, "Well, nothing actually," because he would not be the client but a perfect stranger instead.

She looked about the café. There were several places to sit in the indoor part, and these were all empty. Outside, spilling onto the pavement that ran alongside the parking lot, there were more tables, and these were mostly occupied: a young couple, completely self-absorbed; two middle-aged women with shopping bags at their feet; two teenage girls discussing a photograph one of them was holding—of a boy, no doubt—and highly amused by something—by the boy, of course; and a man sitting by himself. She knew immediately that he was her client and, as he looked up, he knew that she was Mma Ramotswe.

She made her way to his table.

"Mma Ramotswe?"

She reached out and they shook hands.

"Mr. Moeti. *Dumela,* Rra."

There were the usual enquiries of the formal greeting, while she sat down. He had risen to greet her and sat down too, awkwardly, even furtively. Nervousness, she thought. And then, looking for the first time into the eyes of her new client, she saw something else, and that was fear.

It surprised her at first, because this Moeti was a large man, not in girth but in height, and she never expected tall men to show fear. As the waitress came over to take their order, Mma Ramotswe noticed further things about Mr. Moeti: she looked at his shoes and saw that they were well polished, but with a fine layer of dust that had settled since he put them on that morning; she saw the well-pressed khaki trousers, and the two pens in the top pocket of his shirt. So he was a farmer, but he had not been born to it; she was sure of that.

But there was still the fear: that was the predominant impression, and it intrigued and troubled her.

She opened the conversation brightly. "You found this place all right, Rra. I like coming here. You can see everybody." She made a gesture towards the car park. "These big shops are not like the markets we used to have, are they? So we need places like this instead."

He looked out over the car park. Forty-five, she thought. Maybe fifty; old enough to remember how things used to be.

"Yes," he said. "It is a good place."

"And you can talk here," she went on. "The tables are far enough apart to do that. Nobody can hear, except those two girls over there, perhaps, and they would not be interested in what we have to say—their heads are full of boys."

He glanced in the direction of the girls; the photograph was still coming under intense scrutiny. He turned to Mma Ramotswe and smiled weakly. "And their phones," he said.

"Ah," said Mma Ramotswe, "their mobile phones. Yes, that is a big problem, isn't it? So much talking going on. The air above Botswana must be almost full by now with all these words."

He looked down at the ground.

She leaned forward. "I can tell that you are anxious, Rra." She wanted to say that he was frightened, but decided that to refer to anxiety, rather than fear, was more polite—at this stage.

He kept his eyes fixed on the ground. His hands were clasped together on his lap; now she saw them tighten involuntarily. "It is not easy to talk about some things," he muttered.

"Of course it isn't, Rra. I know that. I have many people who come to me who find it very hard. I understand that very well." She paused, watching the effect of her words. "But do you know something, Rra? Talking about it—just saying a few words—is often enough to help. Words can make big things little, you know."

He lifted his gaze. There was still fear in his eyes, she thought; every bit as much fear as there had been at the beginning of their meeting.

"I am a farmer," he said quietly.

"Yes?"

She waited for him to say something more, but he was silent.

"You told me that you lived just south of town," she prompted. "But you did not say where."

"Over there," he said, indicating vaguely. "It's off the Lobatse road. Half an hour."

"Cattle?" she asked.

"Of course." Everyone had cattle, Mma Ramotswe included.

"I was not always a farmer," he continued. "I worked for many years with a mining company. I was in charge of recruitment."

She nodded. "My father was a miner . . . over on that side." She inclined her head in the direction of South Africa.

"That was hard," he said.

"Very. But he came back to Botswana. Then he became late." She realised that she had, in these few words, summed up the life of the man who meant more to her than any other. Yet anybody's life story could be told in such a way, her own as much as anyone else's. She had married a bad man and then been abandoned. She had lost her baby. She had loved her father, and when he died she had opened a detective agency. She had married again, this time to a good man. That was her life in a few sentences.

He started to talk again. "I was left some money by my uncle, and I had also saved hard. So I had enough to stop working for the mining company and buy a small farm. It is not bad land—not the best, but it is good enough for me. We—that is my wife and I—were very happy with it. I bought some cattle and have been living down there."

She nodded encouragingly. It was the commonest dream in Botswana: a small patch of land to call one's own and a herd of cattle. A man who achieved that had achieved everything. Of course it was beyond the reach of most, and sights were lowered accordingly. A share in a small herd of cattle, even half a cow, was as much as many could aspire to. She had been in a room once, a single room lived in by a family struggling to survive financially, and had seen, pinned on the wall, a grubby photograph of a cow. She had known immediately that this was the family's most precious possession—the thing that transformed that mean room into a home.

"So I have had some cattle," Mr. Moeti went on. "Then one died."

"I am sorry, Rra."

"Thank you." He went on: "It did not die of any disease, Mma. Its legs were cut. Like this." He made a sawing motion against his wrist. "It went down on the ground and I found it the next morning. This thing, you see, happened at night."

This thing happened at night. The words made her shiver.

"And then, a week or so ago, it happened again. Another beast down. Same reason." He looked at her. "Now you see, Mma, why I am anxious. That is the thing that is making me anxious."

"Of course. Oh, Rra, this is very bad. Your cattle . . ."

"And it could get worse," he muttered. "If somebody cuts the legs of your cattle, then might they not cut your legs too?"

She was quick to reassure him. "Oh, I don't think so, Rra."

"Don't you, Mma?" There was a note of desperation in his voice. "You may not think that here in the middle of Gaborone, in this place with all its sunlight. But would you say that at night, out at my place, where the only light at night is the light of the moon and stars? And they can't help you, Mma. The moon and stars are no help."

She made a conciliatory gesture. "No, you're right, Rra. I can see why you are frightened." She paused. Why had he come to her, rather than to the authorities? "You have been to the police?"

He shook his head. "What can they do? They will say to me: somebody has killed your cattle, and then they will go away. How can they do anything more than that?"

It was a common view, even if a misguided one. The Botswana Police did act, and the courts did work, even if in other, less fortunate countries one might not be able to say the same thing with great conviction. "They might be able to—if you gave them some idea of who was doing it."

His response came quickly. "I can't. I have no idea."

"You have enemies, Rra? Enemies from the past? Mining enemies?"

He appeared not to have expected this suggestion, and he frowned. "Why would I have enemies from mining? I was just the man who did the recruiting. I had nothing to do with what happened in the mines."

"No, I suppose you didn't. I just think that it's important to consider who may have a reason to do this to you. Is there anybody like that?"

It is hard, she thought; it is hard for us to think of people who dislike us because none of us, in our heart, believes that we deserve the hate of others.

He shook his head. "I have no idea, Mma. And that is why I

have come to you. You are the one to find out these things and save my cattle. I am asking you to do that, Mma Ramotswe, because everybody says that you are the lady to help people."

YOU ARE THE LADY *to help people.* The words came back to her as she made her way home that evening. It was pleasing to know that people thought that of you, but worrying too. You could not help everybody—nobody could—because the world was too full of need and troubles, a wide ocean of them, and one person could not begin to deal with all that. And yet, even if you were just one person, and even if you could never solve everybody's problems, when somebody came to you and looked frightened, you could not say, *Go away, I cannot do anything for you.* You say, instead, *Yes, I will do what I can.* And then, when you go home from work at the end of the day, you sit on your small verandah watching the day turn to dusk, nursing a cup of red bush tea in your hands, and wonder what on earth you can possibly do to help.

CHAPTER FOUR

RICH PEOPLE HAVE MANY CATTLE

THAT EVENING was one of the nights in the week that Phuti Radiphuti, proprietor of the Double Comfort Furniture Store, came to eat dinner at the modest rented house of his officially betrothed fiancée, Grace Makutsi, associate detective at the No. 1 Ladies' Detective Agency. Their dinner arrangements had changed since the accident in which Phuti had lost his right foot and a small portion of his leg. Rescued from the clutches of his jealous aunt, during the rest of his recuperation he had been looked after by Mma Potokwane, who had found him a spare room in the back of her home at the orphan farm. At first Mma Makutsi had come to see him at the Potokwane house and had meals with him there, but this arrangement was never entirely satisfactory from her point of view.

"It's not that I don't like Mma Potokwane," she had said. "She is a very great lady—one of the greatest ladies in Botswana. But . . ."

"You do not need to say it," said Phuti. "She is also a very bossy lady. A good but bossy lady. I think there are many people like that."

Mma Makutsi smiled. "Yes. Have you noticed how she tells us

to eat up after she has put the food on the table? It is as if she is talking to one of the children. 'Eat up now—leave nothing on your plate.' Have you noticed that?"

Phuti had. "And she even told me the other day that I could have another piece of cake if I was good. I think she forgets that we are adults."

"I think that maybe the time has come for us to have dinner at my house again," said Mma Makutsi. "Do you think that you can drive yet?"

Phuti had shaken his head. He did not yet feel able to do that, he explained, although he hoped that it would not be long. The prosthetic foot he had been provided with by the hospital was taking a bit longer than he had imagined to get used to, and it would be a few weeks, he felt, before he could drive his car again. "But I have somebody from the furniture store who can drive me. He is one of our regular drivers, and we can transfer him from those duties. He is a very safe driver—you will not be worried."

Mma Makutsi had been not so much worried as impressed. Having a driver whom one could casually allocate to new duties was something that seemed to belong to an entirely different world, to a plane of existence of which she had only the slightest inkling. She knew that the Radiphuti family was well-to-do, and she knew that when she and Phuti were married her life would change in certain respects, but she was not yet used to the idea.

"He will drive you all the time?" she asked.

Phuti shrugged. "Yes, if I want that."

If I want that. That, she had thought, was the difference. She had never really been in a position to have what she wanted, and now . . . She imagined what it would be like. If you saw a pair of shoes, you could simply take out your purse and buy them. If you wanted a fridge for your house, or a stove, you could simply go to a shop where they had these things and say, "I will have that one, please. And that one too." She paused. Would she do this? She thought not. Now that she was in a position to indulge such whims, she found that she had no desire to do so, except, perhaps, for the shoes . . . Shoes, of course, were different, and yes, the future looked very positive on the shoe front.

With the driver now available to take Phuti to dinner at his fiancée's house, Phuti had informed Mma Potokwane that he would be eating dinner with Mma Makutsi at her place.

"Is that wise?" Mma Potokwane had asked.

He had looked puzzled, and she had gone on to explain. "You are still recovering from your accident, Rra," she said. "You need very good food."

"But she can make that for me," he protested. "Mma Makutsi is a very good cook."

Mma Potokwane had backed off. "Oh, I am not suggesting she is not a good cook, Rra. It is really just a question of experience. I have many years of experience of cooking for other people. It is not something that anybody can do. Mma Makutsi is a very good secretary, but I do not think that they taught cooking at the Botswana Secretarial College."

He had stood up for his fiancée. "She is an associate detective, Mma," he said firmly. "And she learned to cook at home, not at secretarial college."

Mma Potokwane had recognised defeat. She would never have been bettered in such a discussion by another woman, but Phuti Radiphuti was a man, and Mma Potokwane came from a generation of women that was reticent about arguing with men. "But you will still have breakfast here, Rra?"

"I shall, Mma Potokwane. And thank you for that. Thank you for looking after me so well."

She had smiled broadly. "I have been happy to do that, Rra. And I am so pleased that you are getting better at walking now. Soon you will be one hundred per cent again."

"I hope that I shall not need a stick for much longer."

She hoped that too, she said, although a stick lent a man a certain air of authority. "In my village," she said, "we had a headman who always walked with a stick. He said that it was very useful for beating small boys with if they misbehaved. That is not how headmen conduct themselves these days. Things have changed."

"They have," said Phuti. "It is not good to beat people, I think."

Mma Potokwane had looked thoughtful, wistful perhaps. "Maybe not," she said hesitantly. "Even if they deserve it, maybe not."

DINNER THAT EVENING was a rich oxtail stew made with onions, carrots and mashed potatoes. Phuti arrived at six, and he and Mma Makutsi spent a pleasant half hour sitting at the table waiting for the stew to be ready and discussing the events of the day. Although Mma Makutsi respected the confidentiality of her clients, she did not think that this prevented passing on information to fiancés and spouses, who could be expected to be discreet about what they heard. She knew that Mma Ramotswe discussed her cases with Mr. J.L.B. Matekoni, and she understood why this was necessary. "You have to be able to talk to your husband," Mma Ramotswe had said to her. "If you don't, then everything gets bottled up inside you and pop! it explodes."

Mma Makutsi imagined Mma Ramotswe exploding. It would be like a large bottle of fizzy drink shaken up and then, as she put it so vividly, going pop! "One cannot go pop," she had said. "It is not good for you."

"No," said Mma Ramotswe, "it is not. That is why it's important to be able to talk to somebody."

"Phuti is very careful about these things," said Mma Makutsi. "If I tell him something, he never passes it on to anybody else. He sits there and listens, and then he comes up with some remark that is very helpful. He says, 'What about this?' or, 'What about that?' You know how men are, Mma. They often say 'what about something or other.' "

Now, as she served the oxtail stew, she told Phuti about Mma Ramotswe's meeting with Botsalo Moeti. He listened quietly, and was silent for a moment when she had finished.

"Envy," he said.

She waited for him to explain further.

"Just envy," he said. "That's all."

She had not thought of that. Mma Ramotswe had discussed the case with her on her return to the office, and they had both agreed that Mr. Moeti must have incurred the enmity of somebody who was cruel and spiteful enough to cut the tendons of his cattle; they had not thought of envy. But Mma Makutsi knew all about that; she had grown up in rural Botswana, and knew just how powerful envy could be in the country and in the villages. It was a familiar story.

"Somebody with fewer cattle," she suggested.

Phuti nodded. "Or no cattle at all. Somebody who sees this Moeti doing well and growing fat. Somebody who thinks that it is not fair that he should have what he himself does not have. You know how it is, Grace."

"I do. I have lived in the country. I remember a man having his grain store burned down because he had a much better crop than some other people."

Phuti thought this a very apt example. "And who burned it

down? You don't need to tell me: it was somebody who had a bad crop because they were too lazy to weed the ground or take away the stones. That is the sort of person who is envious."

"So if Mma Ramotswe were to ask Mr. Moeti who is the laziest person in the district, then that will be the person she should look out for?"

Phuti smiled at the suggestion. "That's one way, I suppose."

Mma Makutsi warmed to the theme. "Sometimes the best answer to a difficult problem is the simplest one," she said. "We had a case once when we had to find out who was stealing government food at a college. The answer was the husband of one of the cooks. And how did we find this out? We saw how fat he was getting."

Phuti chuckled. "There you are. It seems that people give themselves away most of the time. They cannot hide things."

"Not from the eyes of a detective," said Mma Makutsi, with an air of satisfaction. "We are trained to spot things, you see."

The conversation moved on to the wedding. A date had at last been set and preparations were being made. The bride price—a tricky issue—had finally been resolved, with a payment of twenty cattle being made by the Radiphuti family to the senior male member of the Makutsi family, Mma Makutsi's father being long dead. The negotiations had been unusually prolonged, that same male person, an uncle with a curious broken nose, having initially made an outrageous demand for ninety-seven cattle, or the cash equivalent, on the grounds that the Radiphuti family was well off and Mma Makutsi had achieved the mark of ninety-seven per cent in the final examinations of the Botswana Secretarial College. This embarrassing demand had eventually been dropped, but only after Mma Makutsi had endured an emotionally draining meeting with her uncle, during which she accused him of threatening her future happiness.

"You cannot ask for that, Uncle," she said.

"Why not? They are rich. Rich people have many cattle. Everybody knows that. And where do they get all that money? From other people—from ordinary people. So there is nothing wrong in getting some of it back."

She had defended the Radiphuti family. "They are rich because they have worked hard. That store of theirs started very small—they have built it up through hard work."

He appeared not to hear. "They can still give some of the money back."

"It is their money, Uncle. They did not steal it. They earned it."

"Rich people think that they can take all the money in the country and put it in their banks in Gaborone. I am just trying to fight back for ordinary people—that is all."

It was no use arguing with him, so she simply issued a threat. "I am not going to stand by and be shamed by this sort of thing. If you are going to ask for that many cattle, then I am going to call this marriage off. I can easily find a poor man to marry."

The prospect of losing the bride price altogether had alarmed him. "All right, I will only ask for twenty-five cattle."

"Twenty."

He had accepted this ungraciously, and the negotiations had resumed. Twenty cattle was still excessive, but it was a figure to which the Radiphuti family could agree.

That done, there was now no impediment to the marriage, and the preparations could begin in earnest. As was customary, there would be two celebrations: one in Gaborone at the home of the Radiphutis, and the other in Bobonong at the home of the Makutsi uncle with the broken nose. Phuti had tactfully offered to pay for both, and his offer had been rapidly accepted by the uncle. "It is right that they should pay for our party too," he said. "With all that money they can easily afford it. I hope that they will give us some new chairs too, for the guests to sit on. We only have four chairs, and there will be two hundred people there. Four chairs will not be enough."

"You must not say anything to Phuti about this," warned Mma Makutsi. "You cannot expect people to give you chairs. I will ask him, though, whether he can lend us some."

"He has many chairs in that big store of his," sniffed the uncle. "He should give us some."

The guest list, as at all weddings, of whatever size, was also proving difficult. On the Radiphuti side there were three hundred and twenty relatives, and that excluded distant cousins who would certainly feel offended if not invited. If this class of distant relatives was included, then the number went up to five hundred and sixteen, with a few places being kept in reserve for relatives of whose existence the family was currently ignorant but who would step forward once the invitations had been issued. Fortunately the Makutsi side was much smaller, with eighty-three relatives appearing on the list agreed by Mma Makutsi and her uncle. To this grand total would have to be added friends and colleagues: Mma Ramotswe and Mr. J.L.B. Matekoni, of course, but also Mr. Polopetsi, who still worked in the garage occasionally, and, more controversially, Charlie and Fanwell. Fanwell's grandmother had asked whether she could come, as it was a long time since she had been to a wedding and she had heard a great deal about Mma Makutsi from her grandson.

"All Botswana then!" Mma Makutsi had sighed. "The whole country. Maybe we should just put an advertisement in the *Botswana Daily News* and say that the whole country can come to the wedding and eat as much beef as it can manage. Maybe that is our patriotic duty now."

"People are happy for you, Mma," Mma Ramotswe had said soothingly. "That is why they wish to come to your wedding."

"They like a large feast too," said Mma Makutsi. "And free beer. That may be another reason why everybody wants to come."

She and Phuti talked about the guest list that night after the oxtail stew had been finished and the plates cleared away. Then Phuti raised the issue of the wedding dress. "You can have whatever you like, Grace," he said. "There is a woman at the store who knows somebody who makes very fine wedding dresses. You can choose whatever you like."

Mma Makutsi looked down at the floor. She did not like to ask Phuti for money, and had been worried about the dress. "You will speak to this person?" she asked. "You will discuss the money?"

He had sensed her embarrassment and had reached over to take her hand. "Of course I will. I will tell her that I will pay the bill."

"And shoes . . ."

"You will certainly need special shoes," said Phuti.

"Mma Ramotswe has spoken about a pair she saw today. She said she thought they would be ideal—if they have them in my size."

"Then you must buy them," said Phuti. "Get them soon. Tomorrow, even. The wedding date is coming soon."

She could not restrain herself, and leaned forward and kissed him on the cheek. He seemed taken aback, and she heard him gasp. She pulled back, unsure of herself. She suddenly felt worried. Phuti had never been physically demonstrative with her. She had put this down to shyness on his part, something to do with his stutter, but now the thought crossed her mind: there were some men for whom the problem ran deeper. What if Phuti were to prove to be such a man?

There were no words in the vocabulary of polite Botswana to express such an intimate matter. Women spoke among themselves of such things, and perhaps men did too. But it was not a subject that a couple like Mma Makutsi and Phuti Radiphuti could easily broach. Perhaps she could ask Mma Potokwane about it. It was too awkward a subject to raise with Mma Ramotswe, but Mma Potokwane was, after all, a qualified matron and had trained as a nurse—even if many years ago—at the Princess Marina Hospital. She would be able to speak to Phuti about such matters, perhaps, and make sure that everything was all right.

Yes, she would ask her.

CHAPTER FIVE

YOU KNOW A GIRL CALLED PRUDENCE?

IT WAS STRANGE, thought Mma Ramotswe, that you could go to sleep thinking one thing, and awake the following morning thinking quite another. And so it was with the question of Charlie.

"I've changed my mind, Mma Makutsi," she said in the office the following day. "We need to tackle Charlie. So let's not put it off. You speak to him today."

Mma Makutsi needed no encouragement. "I am ready, Mma," she said. "I will speak to him, but it will not just be me speaking."

Mma Ramotswe asked her what that meant. It would not just be her speaking, Mma Makutsi reiterated; it would be all the women of Botswana. "I shall be speaking on behalf of all the women of Botswana who have been let down by men," she proclaimed. "On behalf of girls whose boyfriends have pretended that babies have nothing to do with them. On behalf of women whose men go off to bars all the time and leave them at home with the children. On behalf of women whose husbands see other women. On behalf of women whose husbands lie and steal their money and eat all the food and . . ."

As she recited this litany of wrongs, the lenses of Mma

Makutsi's large glasses caught the light, sending flashes like warning semaphore messages across the room. Had a man been present, he would have cowered; as it was, there was only Mma Ramotswe to hear the charge, and she nodded her agreement, even if somewhat awed by her assistant's fervour.

"Don't frighten him too much, Mma," she said. "What you have said is true, but we must remember that Charlie is a young man still and young men—"

"Should not be having twins," shouted Mma Makutsi.

Mma Ramotswe raised an eyebrow. "Yes, Mma, you are right. But he is not all bad. There is something in there that is good—we have all seen it. We need to remind him of his responsibilities. We need to encourage him to take them on his shoulders." She watched her assistant as she spoke; she hoped that the decision to get Mma Makutsi to speak to Charlie was the right one. Her assistant was forceful and could be intimidating, but she was also closer to Charlie in age, and it was possible that he would be more prepared to listen to her than to Mr. J.L.B. Matekoni or to herself.

"I will call him in now," said Mma Makutsi.

Mma Ramotswe asked her whether she wanted her to stay in the room or to find some excuse to go out.

"You stay, Mma. Then you can speak too if he will not listen."

Mma Makutsi rose from her desk, adjusted her skirt, and crossed the room to the door that linked the office with the premises of Tlokweng Road Speedy Motors beyond.

"Charlie!" she called out. "You're wanted in the office."

Charlie came in a few minutes later, wiping his hands. "Better be quick," he said jauntily. "I'm working on a big, big car out there. Major technical problem. Ow! It's no use me trying to explain it to you ladies—you wouldn't understand."

Mma Makutsi glared at him. "Oh yes? So you think that we

don't understand mechanical things. Well, I can tell you, Charlie, there are other things that we *do* understand."

Charlie let out a whistle. "Keep your hair on, Mma. Only a little joke."

"Well this isn't a joke, Charlie," Mma Makutsi snapped back. "You know a girl called Prudence?"

Charlie stiffened. The piece of paper towel on which he was wiping the grease from his hands fluttered slowly to the floor.

Mma Makutsi's voice rose. "Well?"

"Maybe," he said, glancing over his shoulder at Mma Ramotswe. "So what?"

"Maybe?" mocked Mma Makutsi. "Maybe these days you don't have to know people to have babies with them. Maybe you just have to *maybe* know them!"

Charlie was silent. He looked up at the ceiling for a few moments, and then he looked down again. "You shut your face, you warthog! That is none of your business."

"But it is *your* business," crowed Mma Makutsi. "It is your business to look after those twins. It is your business to support them. It is your business to stand by the mother. That is all your business. And Mr. J.L.B. Matekoni agrees." Then she added, "And I am not a warthog."

Charlie looked dismayed. "You've told the boss?"

"He knows," said Mma Makutsi. "He knows. Mma Ramotswe, as you can see, knows. Everyone knows now, Charlie. All Botswana's talking about it. And you can't pretend that it's nothing to do with you. And you know what else?"

"What?" Charlie muttered. His confidence, it seemed, had suddenly deserted him.

"Prudence is going to take you to court," announced Mma Makutsi. "She is going to get an order for you to pay for the twins. And all the other expenses too. That will be for the next sixteen years. And we will all be witnesses in her case. Me, Mma Ramotswe, Mr. J.L.B. Matekoni. Everybody."

"You cannot do that," said Charlie weakly.

"Yes, we can," said Mma Makutsi. "You are caught now, Charlie. There is nothing you can do."

Charlie looked at Mma Ramotswe. His expression was crestfallen, desperate. "Mma Ramotswe . . ."

Mma Ramotswe nodded. "I'm afraid that there is only one thing you can do, Charlie. Mma Makutsi is right. You can go and tell Prudence that you are sorry that you have deserted her, and that you are now ready to accept your responsibilities."

Charlie looked from Mma Ramotswe to Mma Makutsi. The large glasses caught a slanting beam of light from the window and flashed it back in his direction, as the beam of a hunter's lamp may catch its terrified target. Then, quite suddenly, he lurched towards the door and struggled with the handle. His hands, still greasy from work, slipped, but on the third try he got the door open and lunged his way through.

"You cannot run away, Charlie!" Mma Makutsi shouted after him.

"That seems to be what he's doing," said Mma Ramotswe. She looked reproachfully at Mma Makutsi. All that business about Prudence going to court was pure invention; she should have anticipated that her assistant would overdo things.

"I think that I have got him to face up to his responsibilities," said Mma Makutsi, taking off her glasses to polish them.

A moment or two later, Mr. J.L.B. Matekoni came into the office. "Charlie has run away," he said. "He's gone. Right down the road."

"Perhaps he is running off to apologise to Prudence," offered Mma Makutsi, replacing her glasses on her nose.

"I'm not so sure," said Mma Ramotswe.

AFTER CHARLIE'S PRECIPITATE DEPARTURE it was difficult for Mma Ramotswe to concentrate on her work. Mma Makutsi had no such difficulty. She sat at her desk with a certain air of triumph, as judge and prosecutor rolled into one, pleased at the fact that Charlie had been confronted and dealt with so satisfactorily. The women of Botswana, her sisters in suffering, had been vindicated in those few well-chosen words delivered to Charlie, who had, in the whole business, been standing as a symbol—some might have said scapegoat—for centuries of accumulated male wrongdoing. Well, women had now had their say, through her lips; they had been given their day in court and had seen the defendant roundly and conclusively vanquished. There was nothing to regret in all this—it was simply a victory to be celebrated. Mma Ramotswe, for some odd reason, was silent, sitting at her desk somewhat morosely. Well, thought Mma Makutsi, her employer had always been too soft on Charlie—perhaps she was now feeling a bit sorry for him.

"Are you upset over something, Mma Ramotswe?" asked Mma Makutsi.

Mma Ramotswe looked up from the account ledger. It was time to send out bills, a task that she did not relish at the best of times, let alone now, in the aftermath of this furious row with Charlie. "A little upset," she confessed. "As you may know, Mma, I don't like conflict. It . . . it disturbs the air."

Mma Makutsi thought about this. "I see," she said. "You heard him call me a warthog? Did you hear that, Mma?"

Mma Ramotswe sighed. "Yes, I heard that."

"He has called me that before. Do you remember that time? He called me a warthog."

Mma Ramotswe did remember. It had been a most distressing

occasion, and she had spoken to Charlie sharply about it, telling him that it was unacceptable to call Mma Makutsi anything, let alone a warthog.

"Do I look like a warthog?" blurted out Mma Makutsi. "Do I deserve such an insult, Mma? For a second time?"

Mma Ramotswe sought to reassure her assistant. "Of course not, Mma. Of course you don't look like a warthog."

"Then why did he call me that?" demanded Mma Makutsi.

Mma Ramotswe began an explanation. Young men used ridiculous insults for no real reason. They spoke without thinking. Charlie might call anybody a warthog; it was probably just the first disparaging word that came into his mind; he did not mean it, and she was sure that he would regret it when he realised that it had caused hurt and offence.

Mma Makutsi listened to this explanation carefully. She took off her glasses again, polished them, and replaced them.

"He meant it," she pronounced.

"Charlie needs to grow up," said Mma Ramotswe. "And he will. It's just that it's taking rather a long time—just like his apprenticeship."

They both tried to return to work, but it was impossible. Mma Makutsi, from feeling pleased with the result of her accusation, now seethed at the memory of the insult; Mma Ramotswe, for her part, felt concerned not only about Charlie, but about Mma Makutsi too. It had not been handled well, she thought—and it was her own fault. She should have taken Charlie aside privately and tried to persuade him to do the right thing; it had been an error of judgement to let Mma Makutsi loose on him like that.

Oh well, she thought; things sometimes did not turn out as we had hoped, and the only thing to do was to carry on regardless. If we stopped and brooded all the time over what went wrong, then we would never get anywhere with anything, and one could certainly not run a detective agency, or any business for that matter, in such a way. The day, she decided, would have to be restarted somehow, if it were to get anywhere.

She looked up at Mma Makutsi. "Mma," she said, "I have been thinking."

"And I have been thinking too," interjected Mma Makutsi. "I have been thinking about this warthog business. When that young man comes back, I'm going to ask him why he called me that, and I will carry on asking him until he gives me a proper explanation."

"I haven't been thinking about that," said Mma Ramotswe. "I've been wondering whether we shouldn't shut up shop for a while. Why don't you go out and look at those shoes I mentioned to you? Try them on. Then go and have a cup of coffee—take the money for that from petty cash. I will pay. We can finish off these accounts some other time."

Mma Makutsi smiled. Mma Ramotswe always had a way of defusing a difficult situation; she never failed. "That is a good way of forgetting, Mma. And you are right—I should not sit here thinking about it and making myself all hot and bothered." She paused. "But what about you, Mma?"

Mma Ramotswe explained that she had work to do that would take her out of the office. She needed to go out to Mr. Moeti's place, and there was nothing like a drive into the country to clear one's head and get the small things of life into their proper perspective. Mma Makutsi agreed with all that, but suggested that Mma Ramotswe was overlooking something even better in terms of distraction and balm, and that was shopping for shoes. She pointed this out to Mma Ramotswe, who laughed, and said that each of us needed to find just the right way to take our mind off our problems, and it did not matter what that was—a drive in the country, an expedition to a shoe shop, a quiet cup of tea under a cloudless sky; each of us had something that made it easier to continue in a world that sometimes, just sometimes, was not as we might wish it to be.

TO GET FROM THE OFFICES of the No. 1 Ladies' Detective Agency to the Riverwalk shops—there was not much of a river, it was admitted by all—you could either take a crowded minibus from the side of the Tlokweng Road, and travel no more than a stop or two, or you could drive—if you had a car—or walk. Mma Makutsi could have asked Mma Ramotswe to take her in her van on the way to the Moeti place, and then to drop her off, but she decided instead that it would be better to walk. She was in no hurry to get back to the office, and a walk there and back would add an hour to the pleasant interlude that Mma Ramotswe had so generously arranged.

She set off a few minutes after Mma Ramotswe, locking the office door behind her and leaving a notice pinned to it saying, *Temporarily closed for investigations.* She had been rather proud of this notice, which informed any prospective client that the detectives were somewhere else on unspecified but important-sounding investigative work. But as she pinned the sign into position, it suddenly occurred to her that a quite different impression might be created, namely that the No. 1 Ladies' Detective Agency was itself under investigation, and consequently had been closed down by the authorities. That would never do, so she reopened the office and carefully typed out a new sign. The wording this time was far better, and, she hoped, quite unambiguous: *Temporarily closed while detective personnel are engaged elsewhere.* That was much better . . . or was it? Could it be read as suggesting that the entire staff of the No. 1 Ladies' Detective Agency was, in fact, working for some other concern? That was certainly not the message she wished to convey, so she inserted a third sheet of paper into the typewriter and typed: *Back soon.* There was no room for misunderstanding there, although there might be some people who demanded, "And what does 'soon' mean, may we ask? How soon is that?" Such people, however, would never be satisfied with whatever one said, and would always be picking holes in even the simplest notice. No, you did not need to worry about people like that.

Satisfied with the sign, she set off. As she reached the road that ran past Tlokweng Road Speedy Motors, a struggling minibus, laden to the gunnels with passengers, and tilting dramatically to one side, started to swerve off the tarmac towards her. The driver had scented the prospect of yet another fare and was gesturing from behind the wheel. Mma Makutsi waved him on, and he resumed his journey in a belch of exhaust smoke. As the minibus went past, she saw people staring at her through the windows: a woman with a purple hat pulled down over her ears; a young girl on her mother's lap, hair festooned with tiny ribbons worked carefully into the tight curls; an elderly man, his eyes closed, snatching a few moments of sleep on the journey. *My people,* she thought. *My people.* And she recalled that when she married Phuti Radiphuti she would never again have to travel by minibus, if that was what she wished. She would have a car, and she would be able to go where she wanted, when she wanted, and would not have others squashed in with her, would not have to put up with the discomfort of the elbows of complete strangers digging into one's ribs, nor, even more disconcertingly, their breath hot on the back of one's neck. That would all be a thing of the past—if that was what she wanted. And she was not sure that it was.

She continued her walk. It was not too hot a day, and a breeze had stirred up from the west, from the direction of the Kalahari, the warm heart of the country. There were people who knew what such things meant, who could read the wind, but for Mma Makutsi it was just a breeze that had sprung up to make her walk to the shops that much more comfortable. She looked up. The sky was without cloud, a dome of lightest blue filled with air, great swirls and eddies of it, which you could see—just about—if you stared long enough. She breathed in deeply, and felt the fine dry air fill her with a buoyant optimism. Life was very good: she had behind her a career that was a success by anybody's standards—ninety-seven per cent, associate detective with several significant and challenging cases solved, a new filing system worked out—a comfortable, if rather small, rented house, and now, to top all these achievements, a well-to-do fiancé who loved her and was kind to her in so many little ways. And here she was with three or four hours of time off—and she would not wish to hurry these things—on a mission to purchase shoes for her wedding.

Nice one, Boss!

Pretending not to notice at first, she began to walk a little bit more purposefully.

Yes, said the insistent, rather chirpy voice. *Put your best foot forward!*

She glanced down at her shoes. She had a few more shoes these days, and this was a workaday pair that she had never paid much attention to. But now they were making their presence felt.

It's smart wedding shoes—with diamonds, we hear. So you'll be forgetting about us, we suppose. Well, we won't be forgetting about you, Boss! Know what we mean?

She decided to ignore her shoes. It was absurd, anyway; shoes could not talk, and it was just a trick of the mind, of the same sort that made one think that somebody has said something when they have just been clearing their throat or humming a snatch of tune. The creaking of shoe leather could produce just the same illusion, she thought, and was probably best dealt with by the application of a spot of polish, or a lick of dubbin.

In your dreams, said the shoes.

She was now at the point along the road where a path led off into a stand of gum trees that had been planted forty years ago, when Gaborone was only a small town. The city had grown, of course, but these eucalypts still formed its boundary at this point; beyond them lay a stretch of rough bush—government land—and then the dam that provided the city with its precious water. It was an odd juxtaposition, as the border zones of towns can so often be. On one side lie the works of man—streets and pavements, storm drains, buildings—on the other is nature, and the transition can be so sudden, so sharply delineated. Here the tar and concrete just stopped without warning, and were no more, their place taken by trees, undergrowth, anthills. And the smells were different too: on one side the acrid odour of cars and hot road surfaces and wafting cooking vapours, which on the other side became the scent of dust and grass and dried bark, and cattle somewhere not far away.

A path led off into this stretch of bush, as paths will lead off in Africa, well defined, tramped bare by passing feet, appearing like dusty veins when viewed from above. These paths knew where they were going, and would meander—never a straight line—turn and twist until they reached some human place, a collection of huts perhaps, a rough wooden stockade for cattle or goats, some place of gathering or labour. Or they would peter out, as if the people whose feet had made the path had suddenly remembered something and turned back, or had just forgotten why it was that they were walking that way and had given up, handing the land back to nature.

Mma Makutsi knew where this path led because she had followed it before on one or two occasions and, taking the right fork after five minutes or so, it had brought her out where she thought it would: near the traffic lights at the corner of the Riverwalk shops. She decided to follow it now because it was easier than walking alongside the Tlokweng Road, with its traffic and its stony surface. The path was more peaceful too, because the only sounds were those of birds and, sometimes, the distant and sporadic ringing of cattle bells; some herds, by ancient right, still wandered among these trees. Occasionally, very occasionally, there might be the sound of some other creature in the bush, the startled cracking of twigs as a small antelope was disturbed—a timid duiker, perhaps, or a little bushbuck. There were many of them over by the dam, attracted by the water that would ensure their survival in the surrounding vleis and low boulder-strewn hills or kopjes, creatures clinging to life in the interstices of a bigger, stronger world.

Mma Makutsi walked on. There was no life about, although she could see from the sand on the path that cattle had been this way not long before. She was thinking of the shoes, and making a mental list of the things she had to find out about them. Colour? Would they go with her dress, which was to be ivory. Comfort? She would have to stand for long periods on her wedding day and at the parties; the shoes should not be too tight or she would feel very uncomfortable. Fabric or leather? Her skin, which was troublesome, did not react well to some synthetic materials, so it was important the shoes have leather lining rather than some sort of plastic. Heels? Again there was a comfort issue—

She gave a start, her heart leaping in fright. A sudden noise; a small crashing sound; something in the bush. Instinct took over, and she took a step back and half turned to run; it could be a snake, a cobra or a mamba, which could be very dangerous if she had walked between the snake and its hole. Mambas loved these old anthills, with their cool chambers and the safety of their darkness, and mambas were so quick, so evil, so filled with old hatred for people.

A warthog. It had come through the undergrowth and now it wandered on to the path, saw Mma Makutsi not far away and for a moment itself froze, as she had. Then, turning round sharply, its ridiculous tail erect like an aerial, it trotted off, back into the safety of the sheltering bush.

Mma Makutsi relaxed. "Sorry," she said after the retreating creature. "Sorry. This is your place."

CHAPTER SIX

A SMALL, INCONSEQUENTIAL BOY

THE ROAD TO LOBATSE runs south from Gaborone, heading straight for a pass that opens through low-lying hills on either side. Like all roads in Botswana, for many of those who passed that way regularly each stretch could evoke its memories: here was where we broke down, by that culvert, and waited for help under that tree—the sun was so hot that day; here we turned off once to visit a distant cousin who lived five miles down that track, so bumpy that we were all shaken up and bruised by the time we reached our destination; here lived a man who kept a mangy lion in a large enclosure; here is the turn-off to Mokolodi; here we bought melons from a woman who had flies swarming about her eyes but seemed unconcerned. For Mma Ramotswe, too, there were memories, going right back; of trips by bus when she was a girl, to see her cousin in Lobatse; of a journey with Note, her abusive husband, who broke her heart and then broke it again; of the time she drove this way with her father, just before he died, and he said that he thought he would never see those hills again but no doubt would find some just like them in that place to which he would shortly go, to that other Botswana just beyond that final darkness.

Mr. Botsalo Moeti had eventually told Mma Ramotswe where he lived. His earlier vagueness on this, bordering on reluctance, had puzzled her. Did he not trust her? Was his fear so great? "A road off to the right," he had said. "There is no notice, but if you look for a large thorn tree beside the road just after Otse, then that is the place; there is the chassis of a very old car in the bush. That is my sign."

She saw the tree, and then the remains of the car. These old vehicles were to be seen here and there—in the dry air of Botswana they barely rusted, but became covered in vegetation and dust and merged with the landscape. Often enough they were beautiful old cars or trucks, tractors too, reminders of a time when such things were built with grace and a sense of human proportion, like the implements to be found in an old kitchen, battered and well used, modest and simple. She had suggested once to Mr. J.L.B. Matekoni that he rescue one of these ancient vehicles some day and tow it back to the garage for restoration. He had laughed, and explained that you could not do something like that; that everything would be solidly fused together now, that the wind would have eroded the cables so that they would turn to dust if touched, that there would be nothing left where once there were dials and tubes and leather seats. The ants would have eaten all those, he said; it would be an exhumation, not a towing. "Cars are just like us, Mma Ramotswe," he went on to say. "When their heart stops—finally stops—then there is nothing left. The life has gone from them. That is true, Mma Ramotswe. That is how it is."

He paused, and then added, "And I do not think they go to heaven, Mma Ramotswe. There is no heaven for cars." He spoke rather wistfully, as such a heaven would be a fine place for a mechanic, surrounded by all the cars that ever were, all those wonderful old cars with their intricate engines and their beautiful, handmade interiors.

He had not meant to be unkind, he had simply wanted to explain the finite life of machinery. Women knew many things, he felt, and there was little, if anything, that he could tell Mma Ramotswe about the world; except when it came to machines. Then, in his view, women seemed less interested; they wanted machines to work, but they did not necessarily want to understand *why* they worked or, more important, why they went wrong. Love was usually quite enough to stop people going wrong, but would not always work with machinery. One of his clients had just demonstrated that. She had brought in her car, which was behaving erratically. "I love it," she said. "I am kind to it. And now it has decided to turn against me. What have I done, Mr. J.L.B. Matekoni, to deserve this?"

"It is not love," he had said. "It is oil."

That is what Mr. J.L.B. Matekoni thought about how women treated cars; but the world was changing, and even as he entertained these thoughts, he began to feel slightly guilty. He was a fair man, who disliked prejudice, but he had yet to be persuaded that women were good with cars. Not that he would ever have dared express such views to Mma Potokwane, for instance, or even Mma Makutsi. These ladies were feminists, he had been told, as he had once informed the apprentices when admonishing them about the things they talked about in the garage, often at the tops of their voices.

"You should watch what you say," he had warned. "What if Mma Potokwane is sitting in the office there and hears these things you say? Or even Mma Makutsi, who has very good hearing? These ladies are feminists, you know."

"What is that?" asked Fanwell. "Do they not like to eat meat?"

"That is vegetarian," said Charlie, scornfully. "Feminists are big, strong ladies. Ow!"

"They are ladies who do not like to hear young men say foolish things about women," said Mr. J.L.B. Matekoni. "They will punish you if you do not watch out."

Charlie had grinned. "If the feminists take over, Fanwell, they will make men sit by the roadside and sell tomatoes. That is their main plan. For you too. That is what is going to happen, big time. Ow!"

Mma Ramotswe steered the blue van off the road. The track—for it was not much more than that—led very quickly to a gate fastened to its post with a twist of wire. She opened this, making sure to close it behind her to keep cattle from straying on to the Lobatse road. That was a major cause of accidents, cattle at night, invisible in the darkness until the last moment when they turned their heads and the driver saw their eyes caught in the headlights, looming large. Everybody knew somebody who had hit a cow, who had lost their vehicle as a result, sometimes their life too.

The track was in good enough condition; a grader, it seemed, had passed along it not all that long ago and had evened out the worst of the ridges and filled the deepest of the holes. This makeshift pact with nature would last until the next rains came, when the dry season's work would be undone with all the quick impatience that nature has for the puny works of man. The first floods of the rainy season were the worst, as the land, parched bone-dry from the winter, would shrug off the sudden deluge, sending it off in red-brown torrents through networks of eroded dongas. Only later would the land drink in the rain and spring to life once more.

On either side of the track, the grey-green bush stretched out, a landscape of struggling shrubs, leaves shrivelled and dusty, filling in the space between the endless forests of thorn trees. The more established acacia provided some cover from the sun, casting pools of shade under which, here and there, cattle clustered, their tails twitching listlessly against the flies. The prevailing note was one of somnolence and stasis, a note taken up and orchestrated by hidden choirs of screeching cicadas: this was a Botswana that had existed since the days when cattle-herding peoples first came to this land; this was a Botswana that was a hundred years from the world of Gaborone, from the world of cars, of white buildings, of commerce and diamonds. But it was the real heart of her country, the heart that she hoped, when her time came to leave this earth, she would see, in her mind's eye at least, before the final darkness set in. And for all that she belonged to Gaborone, and to that other world, Mma Ramotswe belonged here too, and felt beside her quite strongly the presence of her father, the late Obed Ramotswe. As she gazed out through the tangle of acacia, she felt he was there, seated beside her in the van, his familiar old hat resting on his lap, looking out at the cattle and rehearsing in his mind the possible bloodlines of these beasts he knew so well.

Her reverie ended as the van encountered a particularly deep pothole, teetering for a moment before toppling over the rim of the miniature void. Forward momentum prevailed, and the van was soon back on the level, but the creaking and protest from somewhere under the engine made Mma Ramotswe wonder how her white van would have coped with the challenge—not as well, she suspected.

The track changed direction; now came the first signs of human activity: a dip tank, rust-red, with an empty drum lying by its side. The sight brought back a memory—the stench of the dip, that harsh chemical smell, not unlike a mixture of tar and vinegar, which she remembered from her father's cattle post all those years ago. It was an unpleasant smell in itself, but tolerated, perhaps even hankered after, for its association with cattle, and with the life that was led about cattle. Beyond the dip tank there was a rickety enclosure made of stakes of rough-hewn wood—the trunks of small trees—driven into the ground and tied together with wire and strips of bark. Again, this prompted recollections of those long weeks spent out on the lands and at the distant cattle posts, and of the sound of the cattle lowing in the night when disturbed by some movement in the bush: some pair of eyes betraying the presence of a hyena or jackal.

Then she saw the house, standing beside a large thorn tree that had thickened considerably, its upper branches making a dense crown, like a head of unruly hair among the ranks of the well-barbered. It was not an imposing house, but it was more than the single-room structures that served many who lived out in the bush. The roof, like the roofs of almost all farmhouses, was made of corrugated iron, bolted on and painted red. This covered not only the main part of the house, but the shady verandah that ran the length of the front, the space between the whitewashed pillars gauzed in against flies. Behind the house, in a cluster several hundred yards away, was a small group of buildings that made up the servants' quarters. There were always such dwellings—the abode of the cook, or the man who tended the yard, or the woman who did the washing and ironing; so normal and unexceptionable as to attract no attention, the places where lives were led in the shadow of the employer in the larger house. And the cause, Mma Ramotswe knew from long experience, of deep resentments and, on occasion, murderous hatreds. Those flowed from exploitation and bad treatment—the things that people would do to one another with utter predictability and inevitability unless those in authority made it impossible and laid down conditions of employment. She had seen shocking things in the course of her work, even here in Botswana, a good country where things were well run and people had rights; human nature, of course, would find its way round the best of rules and regulations.

As she nosed the van into a patch of shade under the large

thorn tree beside the house, the thought came to her that the solution to Mr. Moeti's problem might be simpler than he imagined. It always surprised her that people could be so blind to the obvious; that a person could mistreat a servant and then show surprise when the one they abused hit back. She had seen this time and time again, and she had even thought of writing to Clovis Andersen and proposing a new rule for inclusion in a future edition of *The Principles of Private Detection.* This rule would state, quite simply: *If you are looking for somebody who hates your client, then first of all look under the client's own roof.* And now, getting out of the van and looking over towards the house, she studied the red iron roof under which, perhaps, resentments were burning. The roof looked back at her, impassive and tight-lipped under her suspicion, and she remembered a proposition that was already included in Clovis Andersen's great work which was just as pertinent to this situation as was any suggestion of hers: *Don't think you know all the answers,* Mr. Andersen had written, and had gone on, with admirable economy, to explain why this should be so: *because you don't.*

A figure appeared on the verandah. Smoothing out the creases in her dress, Mma Ramotswe walked towards the house. The figure now revealed itself as a woman, clad in a dull shift dress over which an old blue gingham apron had been donned.

Mma Ramotswe called out the universal greeting of the Tswana world—"*Dumela,* Mma"—and the woman responded appropriately, though in a rather strange, high-pitched voice.

"I have come to see Mr. Moeti. Is he in the house?"

The woman nodded. "He is sleeping."

Mma Ramotswe looked at her watch. "He said I should come."

The woman looked at her blankly. "But he is sleeping, Mma. He cannot talk if he is sleeping."

Mma Ramotswe smiled. "No, nobody can do that. But perhaps he would like you to wake him up."

The woman shook her head. "Men do not like to be woken up, Mma. Sorry."

Mma Ramotswe frowned. There was something strange about this woman, a deliberate obduracy that went beyond the reluctance of a servant to disturb an employer. She wondered: *Is this her? Is this the one?* That might seem impossibly simple, but Mma Ramotswe had often found a culprit on very first enquiry. People gave themselves away, she thought; they so often did. Guilt shone out of their eyes like the beam of a hunter's lamp in the darkness. What, she wondered, would happen if she were to come right out and ask this woman: *Why did you do what you did to the cattle?*

"His cattle," said Mma Ramotswe. She had not planned to say it, but the thought had somehow nudged the word out into the open, as a chance remark will sometimes be made against our better judgement. It was true that words slipped out; they did; they jumped out of our mouths and said, *Look, you've let us loose!*

The woman froze. "His cattle, Mma? What of them?"

Mma Ramotswe watched her eyes carefully. The woman's gaze slid away, off to the unruly thorn tree. Guilt. Unambiguous guilt.

"He has had some trouble with his cattle, Mma. I have come to sort it out. To get to the bottom of it."

The woman's eyes moved. She was looking at Mma Ramotswe again, and the fright that had greeted her initial remark had been replaced by a look of blankness. "I can wake him up if you like, Mma."

"A good idea," said Mma Ramotswe.

SHE WAS READY to detect in Mr. Moeti's expression the fear that she had seen before, but it was not there, at least to begin with. She met him on the verandah, where he shook hands with her and invited her to sit down on a traditional Tswana chair. The supports of the chair were made of panga panga wood; leather thongs, threaded carefully in a criss-cross pattern, formed the seat and back.

"A good chair, Rra," she said. "A village chair."

He smiled at the compliment. "I have always had chairs like that," he said. "They belonged to my father, who was a village headman, and they came to me when he became late. Now there is only one—the other one was sat in by a very heavy person, one of the fattest men in the country, I think, and it collapsed."

Mma Ramotswe did not stir. The chair beneath her felt solid enough, but it certainly had creaked and even yielded a bit when she had put her weight on it. A chair should be able to support a traditionally built person, and that should apply in particular, she felt, to a traditional chair.

"But you haven't come to see me about chairs, Mma Ramotswe," Mr. Moeti continued, seating himself casually on the low parapet of the verandah.

"I came because of your problem," said Mma Ramotswe. She noticed in the corner of her eye that the woman in the apron was hovering in the doorway. "That private problem you told me about."

Noticing the look, Mr. Moeti flashed a quick dismissive glance in the woman's direction.

"That is the woman who looks after the kitchen," he said. "She has been here forever. Most of these people"—he gestured towards the surrounding bush—"were born on this land. I suppose it's as much theirs as it is mine, except . . . except that it isn't."

She looked at him quizzically. "I'm not sure if I follow you, Rra."

He laughed. "I'm not surprised. I didn't put that very well. What I meant to say is that these people—the people who work for me on the farm—were born here. Their fathers worked for the farmer who owned this place before me. Now they work for me. They're fixtures, really."

Mma Ramotswe nodded. She understood perfectly well; the land came with people, and with the stories of those people. And so when somebody bought the land—as people could do, if they had the money—then they bought not only the land but its people too. For the most part, the new owners would understand that, unless they were foreigners who had no idea of the meaning of land in Africa. But Mr. Moeti, a Motswana, would know exactly what obligations land ownership brought; or she hoped he would. If he did not, then he would soon make enemies, and could easily find that his property came under attack. It was only too easy to start a bush fire, to turn a swathe of golden-grassed cattle range into charred stubble; it was only too easy to take a knife to the Achilles tendon of a cow.

"Are there many such people, Rra? Many here, I mean."

He replied that there were. It was difficult to tell exactly how many people lived on the farm, as not only were babies always being born, but there was also movement away to the towns, or deaths. But if pressed, he would say forty people altogether, in three families. These were all related to one another through complex and convoluted genealogies that only the old people remembered, and even they were now forgetting.

"Do you get on well with them?" asked Mma Ramotswe.

His answer came quickly, and unambiguously. "If you think it's one of them, Mma," he said, "then you couldn't be more wrong. I am their friend, and always have been. There are many children named after me. Go to that place where they live, over there by the dam, and call out 'Botsalo,' and then see how many children come running over. No, it cannot be one of them, Mma Ramotswe."

"I did not say it was, Rra," she said mildly.

"You implied it."

She shrugged. "I have to ask questions. I have to pry—otherwise, how would we find out who has done this terrible thing?"

He said that he understood this.

"And that lady in the kitchen?" Mma Ramotswe went on to ask, looking into the house, her voice lowered. "What about her?"

Mr. Moeti hesitated. "That lady is a very close friend, Mma. She is my wife, but isn't my wife, if you understand me."

She understood, but reflected for a moment on his curious way of throwing opposites together—this was the second time he had done it. "You have a wife, Rra? A legal one?"

He pointed. "She is down in Lobatse. She prefers to be in town. She lives here but she doesn't live here, if you see what I mean."

Now it occurred to Mma Ramotswe that there was another suspect: the wife who was a wife but who also was not. If she knew of the other woman, the resident mistress, then might she not try to get even with her husband? Wronged women did not always take it out on the other woman, Mma Ramotswe knew; often they reserved their venom for the man who had let them down. If there was resentment on the part of the real Mma Moeti—the Mma Moeti who was but was not—then she might well take it out on her errant husband's cattle. After all, a man's cattle were his *representatives* in a sense, and any insult offered to them was an insult to the owner; or so her father, the late Obed Ramotswe, had always maintained, though partly, she thought, with tongue in cheek. She remembered how, when she was a little girl, she saw him raise his battered old hat to some cattle beside the road; she had asked him why, and he had explained that they were cattle of a respected man, of chiefly family, and he was merely according him the respect that such beasts deserved. But then he had smiled, and winked at her, and she realised that the remarks of adults might not always mean what they appeared to mean.

There was a silence as Mma Ramotswe digested Botsalo Moeti's disclosures about his wife. She did not approve of such arrangements, but she did not show her disapproval: he was her client and it was not for her to speak to him about fidelity and those other things that the government advertisements spelled out so carefully. If people like him—well-placed men of experience and status—behaved in a cavalier way towards women, then what hope was there for getting people like Charlie to conduct themselves more responsibly?

Charlie: there was another problem, adding to the list of problems she already had. Moeti, Charlie, the sighting of the white van: these were issues enough to interfere with anybody's sleep.

Moeti's stomach now broke the silence with a loud gurgling sound. "Juices," he explained. "I have too many juices in my stomach."

Mma Ramotswe raised an eyebrow. "Juices are a big problem for some," she said.

There was a note of criticism in her voice—just a touch—but Mr. Moeti did not pick it up, or if he did, gave no indication of having done so.

"I'd like to show you the place where the last attack happened," he said. "Are you ready to come with me, Mma, or would you like some water first?"

She asked for water, and he called out to the woman in the house. "Water for this lady, Mma. A big glass. Very big."

She did not blink. Why did he imagine that she would want a

very big glass? Was it because she was traditionally built? If so, then he had no right to assume that a traditionally built person would drink more than a moderate amount of water. Traditionally built people did not necessarily eat or drink more than those of less substantial construction. It just did not follow.

The woman in the apron brought out a glass on a tray. On the surface of the glass were her greasy fingerprints, each swirl and whorl perfectly outlined, as if etched by an engraver. These prints were about the rim too, which, for some inexplicable reason, the woman had contrived to touch. Although Mma Ramotswe was not unduly fastidious, believing that a reasonable degree of exposure to the germs of others helped maintain healthy resistance, she did not think there was a need to handle a glass quite so thoroughly before offering it to another.

"Look at these wonderful fingerprints," she said, as the woman offered her the tray. "How useful for a detective!"

The woman looked at her blankly.

"Mma Ramotswe is making a joke," said Mr. Moeti to the woman, in a tone of condescension. "It is a joke for Gaborone people, not for rural people like you."

Mma Ramotswe turned to look at him in astonishment. This, she decided, was a man who could well have more enemies than she had imagined.

THEY WALKED FROM THE HOUSE, following a path that took them past the servants' quarters and a shed housing a tractor side by side with an ancient donkey-cart. Mr. Moeti pointed to the cart and told Mma Ramotswe how he believed that the old ways of doing things still had their place. "Donkeys don't go wrong," he said. "Tractors do. And the same goes for everything else. An old radio, for example, has very few buttons. A new one? There are so many buttons that you don't know what to do, even if you're an engineer."

"My husband would agree with you," said Mma Ramotswe. "When people bring in their cars these days, he needs a computer to do everything. He says you even need a computer to work out if you've run out of petrol."

In a small paddock not far from the barn, they saw the donkeys in question, three dispirited creatures standing under the shade of a tree, their heads lowered in that air of utter defeat, of dejection, that marks out their species. A young herd boy, aged no more than seven or eight, was standing beside the donkeys, staring at his employer and Mma Ramotswe as they walked past.

"That child?"

Mr. Moeti glanced in the boy's direction. "Just a herd boy. That was his mother back there in the house."

"Does he know anything?"

Mr. Moeti looked at her in surprise. "No. He's just a boy."

"They have eyes," said Mma Ramotswe quietly—so quietly that he did not hear her and had to ask her to repeat what she had said.

"And?" he asked.

"I have found that children—especially boys—see things and can give you very important information. They notice."

Mr. Moeti shrugged. "You can ask him if you like."

Without waiting, he whistled and gestured for the boy to come over. The child hesitated, and then approached them. He brought flies with him, Mma Ramotswe noticed.

"This lady wants to ask you something," Mr. Moeti said. His tone was gruff, and he stared at the boy as he spoke.

Mma Ramotswe bent down to speak to the boy, reaching for his hand as she addressed him. She asked him his name, and he gave it. He was Mpho.

"So, Mpho, you know about this bad thing with the cattle?"

He moved his head slightly—a nod, but a reluctant one. His eyes, she saw, were fixed on Mr. Moeti.

"Did you see anything?" asked Mma Ramotswe.

He was still watching Mr. Moeti, and Mma Ramotswe glanced up discouragingly at the farmer. "Maybe I should speak to him by himself," she said. "It is sometimes better to speak to children on their own."

"No need," snapped Mr. Moeti. "Mpho, you answer the auntie: You saw nothing, right?"

Mpho shook his head. "I have seen nothing, Mma. I know nothing."

"Are you sure?" she asked.

The boy shivered. He looked up at Mr. Moeti again and then lowered his gaze to the ground. "I am sure, Mma. Can I go now?"

She squeezed his hand. "Of course you can. Goodbye, Mpho, *go siame*." They continued on their way.

"That's an odd little boy," Mr. Moeti remarked, smiling. "He stands there by the donkeys half the time, doing nothing, or just playing with stones he picks up."

"He's a child," said Mma Ramotswe. "Children should be allowed to spend their time doing things like that."

"He has cattle to watch. That's what he's paid to do."

She did not reply. The child's fear had been so obvious, and she was surprised that Mr. Moeti had not felt obliged to explain it away. Did he imagine she had not noticed it? And the cause of the child's fear was equally apparent: the herd boy was frightened of Mr. Moeti. He had seen something—of course he had—but he knew that he was not supposed to talk about it. She could find out what the child knew, if she really wanted to; if she had the chance to speak to the child by himself, then it would not be difficult to encourage him to speak. All you had to say to a child was that you knew what the secret was, and it would all come tumbling out. No child could keep a secret for long; they claimed to, but it was usually beyond them.

But of course it was not that simple. If she managed to persuade the child to speak, then he would be even more terrified, knowing that Mr. Moeti might find out. And yet, if the boy had witnessed the incident, he would be able to identify the perpetrator. And if he could do that, then why would Mr. Moeti have an interest in concealing the fact? It did not make sense at all, unless, of course, the child had seen something else altogether—some incident that explained the attack. Perhaps Mr. Moeti had done something to somebody else that had then resulted in the attack on his cattle, and perhaps the child had seen whatever it was that the farmer had done. Or—and this was also a possibility, she had to admit—perhaps the herd boy was simply frightened of Mr. Moeti in general and really had seen nothing. What was it that Clovis Andersen said in *The Principles of Private Detection*? It was in the chapter on establishing facts—a very important section in the scheme of the Andersen opus. *Do not forget,* wrote the distinguished authority, *that although a possible explanation may seem likely, there may be an entirely different cause operating in the background. If Mr. Green votes for Mr. Brown, you may think that is because Mr. Green approves of Mr. Brown's politics, but the real reason may be because Mr. Brown is Mr. Green's brother-in-law!*

Mma Ramotswe had been intrigued by this passage, and had read it out loud to Mma Makutsi one morning when business had been slack. Mma Makutsi had listened intently before asking Mma Ramotswe to repeat it. Then she had asked, "Who is this Mr. Green?"

"He is Mr. Brown's brother-in-law," replied Mma Ramotswe. "I do not think they really exist."

"Oh, I know that," said Mma Makutsi. "But I am asking because there may be another reason altogether. What if Mr.

Brown has told Mr. Green that unless he votes for him he will cut off his nose? What then? That is a possible explanation too."

Mma Ramotswe gave this some thought before replying. "A good point, Mma Makutsi. And it shows that Mr. Andersen is correct. There may be even more explanations than those you think you have. That is very true."

It had been a slightly odd conversation—many conversations with Mma Makutsi could take a surprising turn—but it seemed helpful to remember it now. There could be any number of reasons for the boy's fear of Mr. Moeti and none of them might have anything to do with the cattle incident.

Mr. Moeti now stopped and pointed to a patch of grass at the side of the path. "This is where the last bullock was found," he said. "He was a very fine beast. Strong. White patches on his head."

Mma Ramotswe looked about her. They were, she thought, in a place best described as nowhere, surrounded by thin acacia scrub that stretched out to a small outcrop of hills to the south. Through the trees, though, she could just make out a fence that ran die-straight through the bush. She pointed at this.

"The border of my farm," said Mr. Moeti. "My neighbour is on that side—I am on this."

"And who is he?" asked Mma Ramotswe.

Mr. Moeti did not appear to be particularly interested. "He is just a man," he said. "He has a business down in Lobatse. He comes here at weekends."

She nodded. This was not at all unusual. The ambition of any successful businessman in Botswana was to own land, and cattle, of course. Wealth in the bank was one thing; wealth in the shape of cattle was quite another, and for many, much more desirable.

She sighed. "It is very sad, what happened to your cattle. Very sad. People can be so cruel to animals. They do not think of their suffering, do they? Imagine how painful it must be to have your tendons cut and you just lie there and . . ."

She looked at him as she spoke, and saw that his expression remained impassive. That was interesting, she noted. Most people, when reminded of pain, reacted in some way. They winced or gritted their teeth, or simply looked distressed. But Mr. Moeti did none of these.

"Not good," he said.

"No. Not good, Rra."

He gestured to the patch of grass. "Should we look around?"

She saw no point to doing this, but having gone out there she thought that she should at least look; not that there was anything to see, really, other than a small patch of ground on which something cruel had been done. There were numerous such small patches of ground throughout the world, she thought, and Africa, her beloved Africa, had many of them.

She looked up at the sky. That was the real witness to human cruelty, to all our manifold sorrows—the sky.

Her thoughts were interrupted by a grunt from Mr. Moeti. It was a rather odd sound, and she wondered for a moment whether he was in pain; it was that sort of sound, the *oh* that escapes our lips when a sudden awkward movement sends an electric shock of pain from the back. What if Mr. Moeti were to have a heart attack out here? Would she have to leave him lying on the ground—on the very grass on which the bullock had lain in the embrace of its own pain—and run back along the path to the house? And what would happen then? How long would it be before a doctor could be summoned or an ambulance brought out from Gaborone?

"Are you all right, Rra?"

He muttered something inaudible.

"Rra?"

"Come over here, Mma Ramotswe. Come over here."

He was bending over, looking at something on the ground. As she approached, he pointed, the gold band of his wristwatch glinting in the sun as he did so.

"You see that?" he said. "I don't want to touch it before you see it. Look."

She peered down at the ground. There was a small, silver-coloured object, half covered by a dried leaf that had blown across it. She went down on her knees; the ground beneath the meagre covering of vegetation was hard and stony. She reached out and picked up the object. A real detective, she thought, would have used tweezers and immediately dropped the evidence into a convenient plastic bag. But where were the tweezers and plastic bags out here? Or even in the office? She would hardly find tweezers among the rough spanners and wrenches of Tlokweng Road Speedy Motors.

She looked at Mr. Moeti. "A key ring."

He held out his hand. "Let me see it, Mma."

She watched him. "Is it yours, Mr. Moeti?"

He shook his head. "I've never seen this before."

"It is a little thing," she said. "It must be easy to drop something like that."

"Yes," he said. He was staring at her intently. "Mma Ramotswe?"

She took the key ring back from him. "Yes, Rra."

"Was this dropped by the person who did this thing?"

She gestured to the wide expanse of surrounding bush. "This is not a very busy place, Rra."

He looked embarrassed. "Of course. I am not a detective—I am a farmer."

"How did you take the bullock away?"

He pointed towards the farm. "I brought my tractor. I came with my stockman."

"Just the two of you?"

"Yes."

She felt the key ring between her fingers. There was a rough edge to it; it was almost sharp; a small, metal map of Botswana.

"And could this be his?"

He answered quickly: "He has never seen it either."

"Oh? How do you know that?"

He looked away. "I mean that I do not think he has ever seen it. That is what I mean."

CHAPTER SEVEN

A TRUTH ABOUT LIES

MMA RAMOTSWE had told Mma Makutsi that they should close the office while they were out, but had said nothing about coming back. Mma Makutsi was conscientious—one did not achieve ninety-seven per cent in the final examinations of the Botswana Secretarial College without demonstrating responsibility and the capacity for hard work—but she felt, nonetheless, that Mma Ramotswe could hardly have meant for her to go back to the office after her shopping trip. Buying shoes was not a simple transaction; one had to take one's time about it, and it was already noon. If the choosing of the shoes took two hours—perhaps three, with time for contemplation—then there would surely be no point in walking back to the office (another half an hour) only to have to close up for the day an hour or two later. No time and motion expert would think that a good idea; such a person, she felt, would be more likely to suggest going home after the purchase of the shoes in order to be fresher and more energetic for work the next day.

Mma Makutsi had attended a lecture by a time and motion expert in her final month at the Botswana Secretarial College. It had been a riveting talk, perhaps the most entertaining of all the lectures they had received at the college, and she remembered almost every detail of what was said. The expert was a rotund man who had immediately engaged the attention of the students—or almost all of them—by telling them how he performed the task of getting dressed each morning. "I am very efficient," he said, smiling as he spoke. "When I get undressed, I hang my shirt on a hanger straightaway. Then, in the morning, if I am wearing the same shirt—and it is not efficient, I believe, to change your shirt every day, unless it is very hot—then in the morning I back up into the shirt like this, while at the same time picking up my trousers with my free hand, like this, and putting first one leg in and then the other. As I put in the first leg I make sure that a shoe is lined up to receive it when it comes out the bottom of the trousers. In this way, I put all my clothes on at the same time. It is a big saving of time. Three minutes and twenty seconds, to be precise. I have plotted it on a graph and taken the average."

The students had all been impressed—or, again, almost all of the students had been impressed. Violet Sephotho, of course, had pretended to be bemused by it all.

"Big nonsense," she said scornfully as they filed out of the lecture room. "No man gets undressed in the way he says they do. Men do not hang their shirts on hangers when they get undressed."

"Yes, they do," said Mma Makutsi. "I do not think that this college invites liars to become visiting lecturers. He said they do, and I believe him."

Violet looked at her pityingly. "What do *you* know about it, Grace Makutsi? What do *you* know about the way men get undressed?"

And then she had smiled knowingly and flounced away, examining her painted fingernails with elaborate interest.

"She is always talking," whispered one of Mma Makutsi's

friends. "Men run away from women like that. They put *on* their clothes when they see her coming. That is the real truth."

Mma Makutsi would have liked to believe that, but felt that the evidence actually pointed the other way. Men had seemed to flock around Violet the moment she left the front gate of the secretarial college. That was a good place for idle men to congregate, for some reason. There was always a small knot of men at the front gate, pretending to have business there, but hoping only to get a glimpse of, and perhaps share a word or two with, girls like Violet. It was sad, thought Mma Makutsi; surely these men had something better to do, but the truth of the matter was that they did not. In the minds of the men who used to attend at the gate, this was by far the best way they could conjure up of spending their time.

As she approached the shop in the Riverwalk shopping centre, Mma Makutsi remembered that time and motion lecture. Efficiency was, in general, a good goal, but she felt, as she saw the mouth-watering selection of shoes displayed in the window, that this was not an occasion on which it should be practised. *Just in from Pariss* panted an enthusiastic sign. *Pariss*? There was an extra *s* there, she concluded; she would have to point it out to them—gently, of course, but one could not let these things go uncorrected. And she doubted, too, whether these shoes came from Paris; Johannesburg, perhaps, or maybe Nairobi. But if they really came from Paris they would surely be even more expensive than they already were.

She looked for the pair of shoes that Mma Ramotswe had identified. There was a pair placed on a pedestal, and she thought they were probably the ones. She peered at them. They were attractive, yes, and she could see how they might be tempting for somebody slightly older, but they were not quite right. Her eye moved to another pair, and then met the gaze of the assistant inside the shop, who was looking back out at her. The assistant waved; they knew each other and got on well.

Mma Makutsi pushed open the glass door of the shop. "*Dumela,* Patricia. You are well?"

The assistant smiled. "I saw you before you saw me, my sister. I could tell that you were coming in here. Shoes for your wedding?"

Mma Makutsi nodded. "Phuti has encouraged me. He says that I can buy whatever shoes I want. There is no budget on these."

Patricia was impressed. She clapped her hands together like a schoolgirl anticipating a treat. "No budget! He is a very good fiancé if he says 'no budget'! You must marry him quickly, Grace, so that he becomes a husband who says 'no budget.' Such husbands are very unusual. In fact, you usually only find them in museums, they are so rare. Husband museums."

They both laughed. But then Patricia leaned forward to touch Mma Makutsi sympathetically on the forearm. "I heard, Mma. I heard that bad news about poor Phuti's accident. So sad!"

Mma Makutsi thanked her. "He has made a very good recovery. You know that he lost a foot?"

Patricia closed her eyes in sympathy. They had a small box of single shoes in the back of the shop—shoes that had been separated from their twin through theft or bad stock control; would one of these fit Phuti, and thus find a home that way? She wondered whether she should ask, but decided that it might not be tactful, particularly so soon after the accident; perhaps later she might say, "Mma, there are some men's single shoes in the back, if they could be of any use . . ." Instead she said now, "Ow! I'd heard that, Mma. That was very bad news."

But bad news should not be allowed to interfere with the business of buying shoes, and the subject was gently changed. Leading Mma Makutsi to the display stands, Patricia gestured to the tempting array of shoes. "Look at this, Mma: Is this not a sight that makes you happy that you're a woman?"

They both laughed again.

"I am always happy I'm a woman," said Mma Makutsi. "Not just when I see nice shoes like this; I think that all the time."

She paused, her eye caught by a pair of black patent-leather shoes with red piping round the sides. They were not wedding shoes, but would be very suitable for wearing to dances—if she was going to go to dances, of course, which was now perhaps rather doubtful after Phuti's injury.

"Being a man is not easy," Mma Makutsi continued. "They are always struggling to prove that they are better than the next man."

"And they have those very rough skins," offered Patricia.

Mma Makutsi had not really reflected on that, but Patricia was right, she thought. Phuti's skin was not all that rough, but there was certainly a place on his neck where it looked as if he had reacted to the razor. Perhaps he should grow a beard. But that would merely exchange roughness for prickliness, and she was not sure which was worse.

"And yet," Mma Makutsi said. "And yet there is much to be said for some men."

"Oh, that is true," said Patricia. "Just as there are some women who are . . ." She left the sentence unfinished.

"Very bad," suggested Mma Makutsi.

There was a silence, finally broken by Patricia. "Such as . . ."

"Violet Sephotho."

"Exactly."

Again there was a silence. Then Patricia said, as if speaking to herself, "Violet Sephotho, the politician."

Mma Makutsi frowned. "Did I hear you correctly, Mma? Did you say, 'Violet Sephotho, the politician'?"

Patricia nodded. "I did. Have you not seen the posters?"

Mma Makutsi had not seen any posters, and now she listened with dismay as Patricia told her about the posters that had appeared in her part of town a day or two previously. These were emblazoned with a large photograph of Violet, under which there was an exhortation to vote for her in a forthcoming by-election. Mma Makutsi said nothing as she absorbed this news. She had heard of the by-election—caused by the death of a popular member of parliament—but she would never have imagined that Violet Sephotho, of all people, would turn out to be a candidate. Violet Sephotho the shameless husband- and fiancé-snatcher; she who at the Botswana Secretarial College had been lazy and uninterested, going so far as to laugh at several members of the teaching staff, and to mock their ways of speaking; she who had achieved barely fifty per cent in the college's final examinations, and yet who had gone on to get glittering job after glittering job (such was the injustice of the world). What possible claim could such a woman have to represent the people of Gaborone?

"I am very shocked," said Mma Makutsi. "It will be a very bad day for Botswana if that woman is elected to parliament. It will be the beginning of the end."

"It will not happen," said Patricia. "God will not allow it."

"God cannot stop everything," said Mma Makutsi. "He is very busy dealing with big things. He cannot watch the results of elections here in Gaborone."

"Then the voters will," said Patricia.

Mma Makutsi pointed out that the voters might not know the full extent of Violet's unsuitability to be their representative. "Not everybody has seen what she is capable of," she said.

"Then we must tell them," said Patricia. "I shall put a notice in the window of the shop saying *Do not vote for Violet Sephotho.*

Many people walk past the shop window every day, and they will see this message."

"Every little bit will help," said Mma Makutsi. "I might make a badge with the same message and wear it every day. And I could ask the Botswana Secretarial College to put it up on the notice board outside the college."

This idea appealed to both of them, and indeed there were others, of varying degrees of practicality. The placing of a notice in the shop window seemed possible, but Mma Makutsi was less sure about the Stop Violet–sponsored half-marathon, or the Violet Sephotho Prevention charity concert in the football stadium. "These are all interesting ideas," she said to Patricia. "But I do not think that we can do them all. For the time being we should just try the notice in your window."

Mma Makutsi now pointed to a pair of shoes near the top of the display. They were white, with a distinct satiny sheen, and had straps crossing at the ankle. She knew immediately that these were the shoes in which she would be married. The knowledge was a relief in a way, as it put an end to doubt, and having the right shoes—as these undoubtedly were—would make everything else, including the dress and handbag, fall into line.

Patricia reached forward and plucked one of the shoes from the display. "I knew it, Mma!" she exclaimed. "I knew that these would be the ones you chose. I didn't want to say anything, because I did not want to interfere, but I knew in my heart, Mma, that these would be the right shoes for you."

She handed the shoe to Mma Makutsi, who took it gingerly, as one might take possession of a great treasure, an item worthy of religious awe.

"Oh, my . . . ," Mma Makutsi muttered, as she examined the shoe. "This is a beautiful shoe."

"A very beautiful shoe," said Patricia. "And do you see that rose,

Mma? We have no other shoes, not one pair, that has a rose on the front. It is very rare."

Mma Makutsi touched the small leather rose; it was supple, soft, and dyed perfectly white, even on the underside of its petals. "So pretty," she whispered.

Patricia lowered her voice. "They will suit you, Mma. You are a very beautiful lady and you deserve these shoes."

Mma Makutsi looked away. She did not think that she was beautiful. She would like to be beautiful—when she was a young girl she had wished for beauty with all her heart, but had become reconciled to the fact that beauty was a gift conferred in the crucible of one's mother's womb and was not on offer at any later stage. But to hear Patricia say it made her wonder, for a moment or two at least, whether it was indeed true; whether beauty had somehow crept up and settled upon her, as age, or the signs of worry, might do.

Patricia consulted a screen to see if the shoe was in stock in the right size. It was, and she retreated into the back of the shop to retrieve the box. Returning a few minutes later, she took the shoes out with a flourish and indicated to Mma Makutsi that she should sit down to try them on.

The ankle straps were fastened with a small silver buckle, which Patricia did up with the facility of one with long experience in such things. "There!" she said, stepping back to survey the effect. "Now stand up, Mma, and see how the shoes feel. They mustn't pinch anywhere, or you will limp down that aisle, and that would never do." For a moment a picture flashed into her mind of Mma Makutsi, her large glasses flashing in the light from the church windows, limping down the aisle with Phuti, still feeling the effects of his injury.

Mma Makutsi stood up. The shoes had reasonably high heels, but they were not meant to be walking boots, after all, and she was accustomed to heels even higher than these. Not, of course, that she wore heels as high as those favoured by Violet Sephotho, who could be toppled, she always felt, brought down with just one judiciously timed push. Violet Sephotho! She did not want to think about that woman at a time like this, but the thought of her as a member of parliament made the back of her neck feel warm with resentment. Members of parliament could become government ministers, and that would be even worse: Violet Sephotho, Minister for Cosmetics and Husband-stealing, perhaps.

"Well, Mma? How do they feel?"

She told Patricia that the shoes were comfortable enough and that she would take them. If they could be put aside, then Phuti Radiphuti would call in later to pay for them, as he had promised.

Patricia looked over her shoulder. She was the assistant manager, not the manager, nor the owner, and her discretion was limited. But everybody knew who Phuti Radiphuti was, and was well aware that he owned the Double Comfort Furniture Store. If credit could not be provided to the fiancée of such a man, then it could be provided to nobody. "I know I'm not meant to do this," she said, "but I think it will be perfectly in order for you to take these shoes now, Mma. Phuti can come in tomorrow, or even the day after that. We trust you."

Mma Makutsi was on the point of saying that it did not matter to her if the shoes remained in the store, but then it occurred to her that it would be useful to break them in before wearing them in earnest. There was walking to be done at a wedding, and standing too, as you talked to relative after relative, friend after friend.

"Thank you, Mma," she said. "I think I'll wear them in."

Patricia looked surprised. "Are you sure, Mma? There is some rough ground round here, even in the parking lot. I've seen people break heels out there. Snap. No heel any more."

Mma Makutsi thanked her for the warning. "I shall be very careful," she said. "I shall watch where I'm putting my feet."

Patricia took Mma Makutsi's old shoes and wrapped them respectfully in tissue paper before putting them in a box. Mma Makutsi watched her friend at work; it was a vocation, this, almost akin to being called to higher secretarial office, or being, as she herself was, an associate detective. Patricia clearly treated shoes with respect, and this extended to tying the box up with string so that it could be more easily carried.

Her task completed, Patricia handed the box to Mma Makutsi. "I'll give you the invoice some other time, Mma," she said. "I haven't got the book. I'll make it out to Mr. Radiphuti, if you like."

Mma Makutsi indicated that this would be exactly the right thing to do. She felt slightly awkward about having the invoice made out to Phuti, but she reasoned that this would be happening a great deal in the future and she might as well get used to it. Then, sitting down on one of the fitting stools, she slipped into the new shoes.

It was an incomparably pleasant experience. The leather of the linings was as soft and as smooth as silk; it caressed the feet. And yet at the same time there was that firmness, that confidence of construction that new shoes have. The leather would yield, of course, but for the moment it was a great pleasure for her feet to be supported in this way.

She said goodbye to Patricia and left the shop. She could not help but look down at her feet as she walked, noticing the sharp contrast between the pristine white leather and the well-worn concrete of the walkway. It was the white leather roses that made the shoes so undeniably beautiful, she thought. Beside them, other shoes, the shoes of passersby, looked mundane and shabby in their lack of adornment.

Yes, came a voice. *We're special. You look after us, you hear!*

It was the shoes talking—she was sure of it. She had, of course, heard enough from footwear as to be ready for this sort of thing, but what struck her about these shoes was their confident, almost cocky tone. It was not for shoes to tell their owners what to do, she felt, so she simply ignored them.

You hear us, hey?

She continued to ignore them, and the shoes fell silent.

She was now in the car park, and was heading over towards the Tlokweng Road, where she could flag down one of the crowded minibuses that plied their trade between the outlying suburbs and the centre of town. The lot was busy, and Mma Makutsi had to dodge several vehicles making their way out of parking places: a wide, gold-coloured Mercedes-Benz purred past her, its pampered occupants looking out on the world with that odd mix of disdain and boredom that seems to afflict the wealthy; a pickup truck heavily laden with crates of beer, two smiling men in the cabin; an elderly woman in a small and ancient car, her face slightly familiar—a client of Mr. J.L.B. Matekoni, she thought. And then, suddenly, a tiny white van.

Mma Makutsi stood quite still. The van, which had been manoeuvred out of a narrow corner, now turned and began to drive between two rows of parked cars. For a few moments Mma Makutsi stared in silence, paralysed in her astonishment. Then she snapped out of her inaction and waved wildly, trying to attract the driver's attention. There was no doubt in her mind that it was Mma Ramotswe's old van. That van had a dent at the back, just above the number plate, where Mma Ramotswe had once hit a post down at Mokolodi—the post, Mma Ramotswe arguing, being in the wrong place. This van had a dent in that precise position, and the odds against it being another van of similar appearance were therefore remote.

"Come back!" she called. "I want to speak to you!"

She was heard, but not by the driver of the van, who appeared to be unaware of the gesticulating figure behind him. A couple of shoppers, carrying their groceries out to their cars, looked at her and wondered what was going on, but there was no reaction from the driver.

"Please stop!" shouted Mma Makutsi, beginning to run after the van. "Please stop!"

The van was not travelling fast as the cars on either side of it were packed tight. This meant that it was easy enough for her to gain on it. Now she was only a couple of hundred yards behind, and was struggling to draw breath so she might shout out once more. But just as she opened her mouth, she felt something give beneath her, and she lurched forward, all but losing her balance, almost tumbling over. She saved herself, but not her shoes. The near-fall was caused by the breaking of the left heel of her new shoes, and her saving of herself was at the cost of its right counterpart, which snapped off under the sudden strain.

Mma Makutsi looked down at her new shoes with dismay. One of them felt loose, and she realised that not only had the heel broken, but so too had one of the cross-straps. She looked back up, and saw that the white van was in the course of disappearing round a corner; a moment later it was gone. Her effort, and the loss of her new shoes, had led to precisely nothing.

It was a moment at which one might simply throw up one's hands and weep, and for a minute or two Mma Makutsi was tempted to do just that. But then, taking a deep breath, she bent to remove her new shoes. She would not give up and cry; not Mma Makutsi, who had struggled so much to get where she had got in life, who carried on her shoulders all the hopes and prayers of that family back in Bobonong; not Mma Makutsi, graduate *summa cum laude* of the Botswana Secretarial College with ninety-seven per cent (a mark since equalled by nobody); not Mma Makutsi, the future Mrs. Phuti Radiphuti and associate detective of the No. 1 Ladies' Detective Agency.

Taking her old shoes out of the box into which Patricia had tucked them, she slipped them back on her feet and continued on her way to the Tlokweng Road. One or two people had witnessed the tragedy, or at least had seen part of it: a young man passing by, a boy on a bicycle, an old man standing in the shade of a tree. But they had only seen a woman racing after a white van and then stumbling; they had seen her bend down and change her footwear before walking off towards the main road. So might we fail to see the real sadness that lies behind the acts of others; so might we look at one of our fellow men going about his business and not know of the sorrow that he is feeling, the effort that he is making, the things that he has lost.

PHUTI RADIPHUTI called round for dinner that night, as was his habit. Mma Makutsi greeted him at the door and hung his jacket on the peg she had put up in the kitchen for just this purpose. She was proud of that peg, of the shining brass of which it was made, of the fact that she had positioned it in exactly the right place. She had an eye for decor, she felt, and she was looking forward to decorating their new home, when Phuti got round to acquiring it. Not much progress had been made in house-hunting—indeed, the search had not even begun yet, in spite of the steadily broadening hints she dropped in that direction.

That evening it was Phuti himself who brought up the subject of houses, although perhaps not with the intention of discussing their own situation.

"We sold a very large sofa today," he remarked, as Mma

Makutsi dished out the mashed potato. "It was every bit as wide as this room. I went to the customer's house with the delivery men."

"That must be a sofa for very wide people," said Mma Makutsi.

Phuti laughed. "Actually, they were very thin. He looked like a rake and his wife was not much more than a beanpole. I do not know why they need a sofa as big as that."

Mma Makutsi thought for a moment. "Perhaps they have very fat friends," she suggested. "Or perhaps they want a big sofa because they themselves are very small. Mma Ramotswe has a theory like that about men and cars."

"She has many theories," said Phuti. It was not a sarcastic or unkind remark, of the sort that one might make about an opinionated person; Mma Ramotswe did indeed have theories, and Phuti Radiphuti in general had a high regard for her views.

"Yes," continued Mma Makutsi. "She believes that men who buy big, powerful cars are making up for not feeling big and powerful inside."

Phuti Radiphuti considered this. He knew several people with such cars, and he thought that there was some truth in Mma Ramotswe's observation.

"I like going to see people's houses," Phuti said. "That is why I often go out with the delivery men. This house—the big sofa house—was very nice. Freshly painted. All yellow outside and green inside. It was a very pretty house."

Mma Makutsi seized her opportunity. "There are some very good houses," she said, and added, almost wistfully: "Some of them are for sale, I think."

Phuti nodded. "There are always houses for sale. Many houses."

Mma Makutsi looked down at the mashed potato on her plate. It made a small range of mountains, intersected by rivulets of dark brown gravy. An ant, she thought inconsequentially, might look on this and think it was a whole country.

She looked up. "Of course, when there are many houses for sale then that will be a good time to buy a house. That is what they call the law of supply and demand. We were taught about it at the Botswana Secretarial College. They mentioned it many times there."

Phuti nodded, but only vaguely. "And you?" he asked. "What did you do today?"

"I went—" she began, and stopped. She had been about to tell him about her trip to the shop to buy shoes, but she could not bring herself to confess to the disaster that had occurred. If she could get the shoes repaired, she could tell him then. But for now it was just too embarrassing—and too painful.

Phuti took a mouthful of potato, swallowed, and then wiped his mouth with the piece of paper towel Mma Makutsi had put by his plate. "Yes? You went . . . ?"

"I went to work," she said.

"Ah. And what happened there?"

"The usual thing."

"Nothing out of the ordinary, then?"

"No. As I said: the usual."

He nodded. "So it was a so-so day? Just so-so?"

"So-so," said Mma Makutsi.

There was a silence, and they both set to finishing their mashed potato and gravy. As she ate, Mma Makutsi could not help but remember what Mma Ramotswe had once said about telling the truth. "Not saying something can be exactly the same as telling a lie, Mma Makutsi," she had said. "There are lies you tell with your lips and lies you don't need your lips for. And once people start telling lies, then they become like spiders who weave their web about themselves. They become stuck—caught by the lies all about them. And then they can't get out of the web, no matter how hard they try." Mma Ramotswe had shaken her head in regret over these mendacious unfortunates, and then, as an afterthought, had added, "That is well known, Mma Makutsi. That is well known."

CHAPTER EIGHT

THE EVENTS OF AN EVENTFUL MORNING

HAVING BEEN the first to arrive in the office the next morning, Mma Ramotswe was one cup of tea ahead of Mma Makutsi. It was her second cup of red bush tea of the day, the first having been consumed in the garden of her house on Zebra Drive on her early morning walk-round. She did that walk every day, at exactly the same time, with the result that she was sure the birds she saw were those she had seen the day before, and the day before that. Some of them, she suspected, recognised her and understood that whatever dangers the day ahead held in store for them, this particular woman was not among them. And there were many dangers for birds—from snakes in the trees in which they made their nests to the hawks and eagles that could descend like arrows from the sky above. She remembered as a girl being called by her father to witness a noisy drama taking place in a tree on the edge of their fields near Mochudi. She had heard the birds before she had seen them, as they filled the midday air with strident, high-pitched squawking. And as she and Obed approached the tree, she saw a whole dancing flock of birds, dark little dots against the sky, dipping and darting above the canopy of a spreading acacia.

"Why are they dancing?" she had asked.

"Not dancing, Precious. They are defending their home."

Nearing the tree, they stopped, and he pointed to a dark shape that was the birds' nest. "Can you see it?" he asked. "There—just over there."

She had stared into the tangle of twigs and leaves. There was movement, but she was not sure what it was, until suddenly one of the twigs seemed to unwind itself and move sinuously between two neighbouring branches.

"Yes," said Obed. "That is the snake. And these poor birds can only shout and fly about. They cannot stop their enemy."

She had asked him to throw a stone, to deter the snake from its attack on the nest, but Obed had simply shaken his head. "We cannot do that," he said. "We cannot always stop the things we do not like."

She had been astonished. Everybody threw stones at snakes—it was what people did—and his refusal stuck in her mind. Later, much later, she remembered his words and pondered them. *We cannot always stop the things we do not like.* She knew now what he meant, of course—that nature had to be left to take its course—but she had realised that there was a far greater truth there too. There were some things that one could stop, or try to stop, but it was a mistake to go through life trying to interfere in things that were beyond your control, or which were going to happen anyway, no matter what you did. A certain amount of acceptance—which was not the same thing as cowardice, or indifference—was necessary or you would spend your life burning up with annoyance and rage.

Mma Makutsi might be gently reminded of this, she thought. Her assistant allowed herself to be annoyed by the apprentices—particularly Charlie—and by their feckless ways; it might be better, Mma Ramotswe felt, if she accepted that young men behaved foolishly no matter what anybody said to them, and that the only real cure for that was time and maturity. You could speak to them, of course, you could try to show them where they were going wrong, but you should not work yourself up into an impotent rage when they went off and behaved in exactly the same way as young men always had.

Charlie had come into her thoughts that morning as she walked about her garden. She wondered whether he would be at work that day. He had absented himself from the garage before on more than one occasion, but returned a day or two later, full of excuses, usually relating to family funerals or sick aunts or matters of that sort.

"Just how many grandfathers do you have, Charlie?" Mr. J.L.B. Matekoni had asked once. "If I remember correctly—and you must tell me if I am wrong—you went to the funeral of your grandfather ten months ago, and then again three months back. And now he has died again. This is very sad that he should be dying so much."

Mma Makutsi, who had overheard this reproach, joined in gleefully. "That is very unfortunate, Charlie," she said. "Most of us have to die only once. Once. You are making your poor grandfather die over and over. That is not very kind, Charlie."

On those occasions he had come back, and Mr. J.L.B. Matekoni, who was not only a fine mechanic but a good and generous employer too, had done nothing more than dock a small amount from the young man's pay—not even the proper amount that should have been forfeited, as Mma Makutsi had pointed out.

"Mr. J.L.B. Matekoni, you are too kind to that young man," she said. "He has to learn that no work means no pay. That is lesson number one, as they taught us at the Botswana Secretarial College. *Stay away, no pay; full day, can play.* That is what we were taught."

But Mr. J.L.B. Matekoni had just smiled. "When men are young, like Charlie, the brain is not quite right. It is like an engine that goes smoothly most of the time, but then backfires. That is what is happening. And it doesn't help to lose patience, you know."

Mma Ramotswe thought that Charlie's latest disappearance might be more serious. Although they had talked about the need for him to assume his responsibilities for his twins, she had her doubts as to the likelihood of this. It might have been unwise to put too much pressure on him, as he might just decide—as he probably already had done—simply to move away. There were jobs elsewhere to be had by young men with some mechanical skills, even if they were not fully qualified mechanics. Somebody had recently approached Fanwell with the offer of a well-paid post at a safari camp in the north, and had the young man not been reluctant to leave his family, he might well have seized the opportunity. If Fanwell, who was much quieter and less assertive than Charlie, could attract such offers, then Charlie could certainly do the same. The Okavango Delta, remote as it was, would be a good place for a young man seeking to avoid the demands of a girlfriend with twins.

She had finished her tea and walked back to the house. It was now that the day's work began: the rousing of Mr. J.L.B. Matekoni, who was quite capable of sleeping through his alarm clock; the waking up of the children and helping Motholeli to dress and get into her wheelchair; the preparation of breakfast—these were just the first of the many tasks that the day entailed. And then, of course, there was the office, and the . . .

. . . and the first cup of office tea, which she had almost finished by the time Mma Makutsi came in, put her bag down beside her desk, and started the day with a wail. "Oh, Mma Ramotswe, I am very, very upset. This is terrible. Oh, I do not know what to do—I do not."

Mma Ramotswe rose to her feet, crossed the room and put an arm round her assistant's shoulder. "Oh, Mma, what has happened?"

Mma Makutsi, feeling that perhaps she was being a trifle overdramatic, tried to smile. "I'm sorry, Mma, I didn't mean to make you think the world is coming to an end. No, it is not that bad." She paused as Mma Ramotswe, looking relieved, returned to her desk. "But it is still bad. Very bad."

Mma Ramotswe did not have to prompt her assistant any further.

"I bought those shoes," Mma Makutsi began. "They were not quite the shoes that you saw, but they were like them. They were very beautiful, with white flowers on the front, made of leather, of course."

"Very suitable," muttered Mma Ramotswe.

"I have never seen such pretty shoes before," continued Mma Makutsi. "And they were comfortable too. They were very comfortable."

Mma Ramotswe noticed the ominous use of the past tense. The shoes had been stolen, perhaps, or left behind in a minibus. Anything left behind in a minibus would never be seen again, as Mma Potokwane had once discovered. She had taken a minibus back to Tlokweng one day after shopping in town for a new dress. The parcel containing the dress had been left under a back seat; a few days later she had seen her new dress being worn by a woman standing by the side of the road. She had tackled her about it, of course, but the woman had claimed to have been given the dress by a friend, and would certainly not be handing it over. And if Mma Potokwane wished to take the matter any further, she was perfectly welcome to raise the matter with the woman's brother, who was a policeman and did not take kindly to false accusations of crime being levelled against perfectly innocent persons . . .

Mma Makutsi sniffed. "I wore them out of the shop and I saw . . . well, I saw something and ran after it. And then I tripped and I broke both heels and a strap." She paused to sniff again. "And then I went home and Phuti came for dinner and I did not tell him what happened because I was so ashamed. And now I'm ashamed for not telling him. I am filled with shame, Mma Ramotswe—filled with shame."

Mma Ramotswe waited to see if Mma Makutsi had finished. She understood why anybody should feel upset about such a thing—particularly if shoes meant as much to you as they did to Mma Makutsi—but she had heard of considerably worse disasters than this. She knew, however, that it never helped to tell another that their troubles were eclipsed by the troubles of others, tempting though that might be. If you have a sore tooth, it does not help to be told that there are people with far more severe toothaches. Yet one thing in this story intrigued her: What had Mma Makutsi seen that made her want to run after it? People spoke of chasing a bargain: Had she seen something on sale in one of the shops? For a moment, she allowed an irreverent image to form in her mind of Mma Makutsi, her large glasses catching the sun, running towards a stall with a sign on it reading BIG SALE—HURRY! HURRY!

She banished the picture from her thoughts. "Tell me, Mma, what did you see that made you want to run?"

Mma Makutsi hesitated. "I will tell you in a moment, Mma. First, look at my poor shoes."

She extracted the damaged shoes from her bag to show Mma Ramotswe.

"See? See how beautiful they were, and now . . . Now, they are just rubbish."

Mma Ramotswe rose from her desk to examine the shoes. "This is very sad, Mma, but don't you think they could be fixed? These heels, they could be glued together, and this strap could be stitched. It should not be hard to stitch something like that."

She handed the shoes back to Mma Makutsi. "But what did you see, Mma? What made you run?"

Mma Makutsi replaced the shoes in her bag. "I think I saw a ghost," she said quietly.

There was silence. Then Mma Ramotswe spoke. "In broad daylight?"

Mma Makutsi examined her fingernails. "If ghosts exist, Mma—and I am not prepared to exclude that possibility—then why should they just appear at night? Where do they go during the day, might one ask?"

"I don't know," said Mma Ramotswe. "It would be interesting to find out."

Mma Makutsi agreed that it would. "In this case," she went on, "the ghost that I think I saw was the ghost that maybe you yourself saw only a few days ago—the ghost of your late van."

Mma Ramotswe gasped. "My van?"

"Yes, Mma. It was in the parking lot near the shops, on the Tlokweng Road side. I saw it reversing out of a parking place and I tried to stop it. But the driver did not hear me, and he just drove off."

Mma Ramotswe reflected on this. So the van really was running once more, in spite of Mr. J.L.B. Matekoni's conviction that it would not. And the driver was a man—that was an additional piece of information; as was the fact that he shopped at the Riverwalk shops—another piece of potentially useful knowledge. "I do not think it is a ghost," she said. "It is my van. I had heard that it had been bought by a young man up north somewhere, near the Tuli Block. I thought it had been bought for parts, but he must have changed his mind." She paused; perhaps something about the van had stayed his hand and he had been unable to end its life. "Yes," she continued. "That's what must have happened."

Mma Makutsi nodded. This seemed quite reasonable to her. "Well, you must be happy that it is back on the road, Mma."

Yes, thought Mma Ramotswe, I am. But in a curious way, if the knowledge that the tiny white van had been restored was reassuring, it was also saddening. Some other person—somebody who did not necessarily appreciate the white van—would be driving it while she, who loved it, was driving a new blue van of very little character. If only they were able to change places . . . She stopped herself. The thought had occurred to her on a whim, but now that she thought of it more seriously it seemed so obvious. The person who currently owned the white van would probably very much like to have a newer van. If she were to approach him and offer to exchange vans, he would no doubt leap at the chance.

The idea was a delicious one, and it brought a broad smile to her face.

"So you're happy, Mma Ramotswe," said Mma Makutsi. "You are smiling. That is very good."

Mma Ramotswe brought herself back to reality. It would be ridiculous to exchange a new van for an old one—far better to buy the tiny white van back. She now became aware that Mma Makutsi was speaking to her . . .

"I was thinking of something," she said quickly. "But we should really get back to work, Mma Makutsi, or we would spend our whole day talking and thinking about this and that."

"Yes, you're quite right," agreed Mma Makutsi. She knew, though, that talking and thinking about this and that was exactly what both she and Mma Ramotswe would love to do, but could not, as that brought in a great deal of happiness but no money, and a lack of money had a tendency to diminish happiness in the long run. It need not, of course, and she remembered that she had been happy enough when money had been tight. Now things were different, but she realised that she would have to remind herself of how life had been before. Those who had enough money, she thought, often forgot those who had none. Mma Ramotswe had once told her that, and she had remembered it. "Never forget, Mma," she had said, "that there are people who will be looking at you and wishing to be in your shoes. Because they have no shoes, you see." It was a puzzling comment, and a rather odd one, but now that she called it back to mind she found that she knew exactly what Mma Ramotswe had meant.

BY THE TIME of the mid-morning tea-break, Mma Ramotswe and Mma Makutsi had more or less completed the task of sending out the month's-end invoices. This was a pleasant task—the direct opposite of the business of paying bills, and now that the No. 1 Ladies' Detective Agency was reasonably well established, the invoices always added up to more than the bills to be paid. It had not always been so, especially in the early days of the agency, when there had been the merest trickle of clients and an even smaller number of invoices, given Mma Ramotswe's habit of taking on meritorious cases for no fee. She still did that, but there were plenty of cases that paid well enough to give them both a modest but adequate living.

"That's that then," said Mma Makutsi, as she stuck the last stamp on the final invoice. "Two thousand pula for knowing that your wife is a bad woman. I feel sorry for that man, Mma."

Mma Ramotswe glanced at the envelope. The Ditabonwe case. "Yes, that poor man does not deserve it. He should not have married that woman."

"Three boyfriends," said Mma Makutsi disapprovingly. "And all the time she was living in that expensive house and eating her husband's food."

"And where will the boyfriends be when they discover that she no longer has any money and has been thrown out of the house? Will they be at her side, Mma Makutsi?"

"They will not," said her assistant.

They were silent for a moment, both contemplating the foolishness of others—their bread and butter. Then Mma Ramotswe made a gesture of resignation. "People do not learn, Mma," she said. "But I suppose we must carry on hoping that they will. You never know." She paused, looking at the kettle. "And now, I think, it's time for tea. Would you mind switching on the kettle, Mma Makutsi?"

The tea was infusing in the pot when Mr. J.L.B. Matekoni came in, closely followed by Fanwell. Mma Makutsi, who was lining up the mugs on the filing cabinet, turned and looked the two men up and down. "No Charlie," she said.

At the mention of his fellow apprentice, Fanwell looked down at the floor.

"No," said Mr. J.L.B. Matekoni. "There is no Charlie, is there, Fanwell?"

Fanwell muttered something that none of them could make out.

"Well, Fanwell?" Mma Makutsi pressed. "I did not quite hear what you said. No Charlie, is there?"

"He is not here," said Fanwell. "I am here, but he is not. I am not his boss. I cannot answer for him."

Mma Makutsi glanced at Mma Ramotswe before turning again to the young man. "You know where he is, though, don't you?"

"I do not," muttered Fanwell.

Mma Makutsi shook her head. "I think you do, Fanwell."

Mr. J.L.B. Matekoni, pouring tea into his mug, made a gentle intervention. "I don't think we can expect Fanwell to know Charlie's whereabouts," he said. "You would tell us if you knew, wouldn't you, Fanwell?"

Fanwell thought for a moment. "He asked me not to tell you," he said.

"Ha!" exclaimed Mma Makutsi. "So he told you. You see? I was right. You cannot lie to me, Fanwell. You can't fool a detective."

Fanwell looked to Mr. J.L.B. Matekoni for help. Mma Ramotswe noticed this, and came to his rescue. "You mustn't worry, Fanwell," she said quietly. "Mma Makutsi is trying to be helpful, you see. We don't want to punish Charlie—we just want to make sure that he's all right."

"And make sure that he faces up to his responsibilities," interjected Mma Makutsi.

Mma Ramotswe made a calming gesture. "Mma Makutsi, please . . ."

"Justice," said Mma Makutsi. "That's what I believe in, Mma. Justice for wronged women, that's all."

Mma Ramotswe rose to her feet. "Fanwell, you come with me for a moment. Just come with me." She pointed to the door.

They went out through the garage, past the car on which the young man and Mr. J.L.B. Matekoni had been working.

"That poor car," remarked Mma Ramotswe. "It looks so sad with all its parts exposed like that. And yet you and Mr. J.L.B. Matekoni will put it all together again and it will be as good as new. It's a great skill you have, Rra."

Fanwell smiled with pleasure. "Thank you, Mma. It is easy when you know how."

It is easy when you know how. Yes, thought Mma Ramotswe. It was easy when you knew how, and right at that moment she was thinking of how Mma Makutsi most certainly did *not* know how, at least when it came to dealing with young men.

They went out from under the shade of the garage eaves, out into the warm morning sun; above them an empty sky, so high, so pale, and a bird, a speck of black, circling in a thermal current. Mma Ramotswe took Fanwell's arm and walked with him towards the acacia tree behind the garage. The young man, she noticed, was shivering, as if a cold breeze had suddenly blown up from somewhere; but the air was still.

"You're upset, Fanwell, aren't you? You're shivering."

He nodded almost imperceptibly.

"Why?" she asked. "Are you afraid of something?"

He did not answer immediately, but looked up into the sky. She followed his gaze. There was nothing; *or nothing I can see,* she thought.

"Charlie told me not to tell anybody," he said. "He has come to my place."

Mma Ramotswe nodded. That made sense.

"So he is staying at your place? With your grandmother and the children?"

"Eee, Mma." It was the way that people said yes, and it could be said through an exhalation of breath. It was an eloquent sound, capable of registering a range of emotions. The suggestion here was of regret, tinged with fear.

"It is not right that he should put you in this position," said Mma Ramotswe. "Charlie should not put his problems on your shoulders."

Fanwell turned to face her. "He said he would kill me."

Mma Ramotswe gasped. "Charlie said that?"

Fanwell inclined his head. "He said that if I told anybody where he was, he would kill me."

Mma Ramotswe snorted. "What nonsense! He didn't mean that, Fanwell. You know how Charlie is always talking nonsense. Big words that mean nothing—nothing at all."

Fanwell was not convinced. "He meant it, Mma. He put his fist in my face like this—shaking it about—and then he said that if I told anybody he would come at night when I was sleeping and pinch my nose so that I had no air. He showed me how he would do it."

"Pinch your nose!" exploded Mma Ramotswe. "That is complete, one hundred per cent nonsense, Fanwell. You cannot stop a person breathing like that. If you pinch somebody's nose, then they simply open their mouth and breathe that way. Charlie was joking—he must have been."

Fanwell listened to her, but still looked miserable. "Please do not come to fetch him," he said. "I do not want that. Even if he does not kill me, he will do something bad to me."

Mma Ramotswe reached out to touch him lightly on the forearm. "Very well," she said. "I will not come and look for him."

"And you won't tell Mma Makutsi?"

She assured him that she would not. "But you will have to do something for me," she said. "You must tell him that I have offered to help him. You must give him that message from me. You must tell him that he should come to my house—at night if he likes. He should come to see me and I can tell him how I shall be able to help him."

She waited for the young man to respond, and eventually he did. He would pass this message on to Charlie, he said, and he would try to persuade him.

They walked back to the garage, where Mma Ramotswe left him while she went back into the office.

"Where is he, then?" asked Mma Makutsi. "Did you get it out of him?"

Mma Ramotswe put a finger to her lips. "Subject closed, Mma," she said. "Closed until further notice."

She looked over her shoulder through the open door into the garage. Fanwell was standing next to Mr. J.L.B. Matekoni, looking down at the engine on which they were working. He seemed so slight beside the well-set figure of the older mechanic—not much more than a boy really, with all the vulnerability that boys have. The sight tugged at her heart and she turned away again. She knew that Fanwell supported his grandmother and several of his younger brothers and sisters on his tiny salary as an apprentice. Yet he never so much as mentioned this fact, nor complained about it. This made her think: those who have a great deal to complain about are so often silent in their suffering, while those who have little to be dissatisfied with are frequently highly vocal about it.

CHAPTER NINE

WITH REFERENCE TO THAT PREVIOUS KISS

MMA RAMOTSWE liked to leave the concerns of the office where they belonged—in the office. But that evening, as she drove home from work, following the tree-lined route that she liked to take through the older area of town known simply as the Village, she found herself thinking of the Moeti case. She had done nothing about it that day—there had been other things to claim her attention—but now she found herself considering possibilities. As often happened, the words of Clovis Andersen came to mind. His general advice, applicable to almost all cases, was to talk to as many people as possible, or rather to get them to talk to you. *The more you listen, the more you learn,* he wrote in *The Principles of Private Detection,* and Mma Ramotswe had been particularly struck by the wisdom of these words, even on one occasion drawing them to the attention of Mr. J.L.B. Matekoni. He had frowned, inclined his head, and said, "Well, Mma, I think that is certainly true. You cannot learn anything if you close your ears. I think that is undoubtedly true."

She had gone so far as to work these words into a small needlework sampler that she had embarked upon, the words forming the centre part of the piece, with detailed pictures of Kalahari flowers around the edge, all executed in colourful thread. She had been pleased with the result, and had donated it to the sale of work in aid of the Anglican Hospice. It had sold well, she was told, to the wife of a hotel manager, a woman widely known to be something of a gossip. The humour of this had not escaped the ladies running the sale of work, who had all agreed that the woman in question was contemplating the listening being done by others rather than by herself.

Mma Ramotswe was certainly prepared to listen to anybody who had any light to shed on the unfortunate fate of Mr. Moeti's cattle, but she realised that it was going to be difficult to find that person or persons. It would be different if the case were in some suburb of Gaborone, or even in a village; one could always find somebody in the street with views to express—one of the neighbours usually. But this was in the country, where one's only company as often as not were the birds, or the small creatures that scurried through the bush. There was that boy, she recalled, and the woman who worked in the house. Mpho seemed to know something, but he was clearly frightened of Mr. Moeti—for whatever reason—and she doubted whether she would get anything out of him. Unless, of course, she were able to speak to the boy in private, if she could somehow get him on his own somewhere. Boys could be good informants, as she had discovered on a number of earlier occasions; boys saw things, and remembered them.

As she paused at a crossroads to allow a couple of trucks to lumber past, she considered the chances of a private conversation with Mpho. The boy was the son of the woman who worked in the house, the one she had met, so he presumably lived with his mother in the staff quarters behind the house. She was not sure how old he was, even if she was certain that he was under the age of legal employment; but that made no difference. There were plenty of children who worked on farms, unofficially, and there were even some who worked in towns. *Bobashi* were children whose parents were dead, or who had run away from home and who survived by their wits. They tended to be found in the towns rather than in the country; she had even come across one who lived in a storm-water drain, a scrap of a child with a face that had seemed so prematurely worldly-wise. She had tried to bring the child to the attention of Mma Potokwane, but when she had driven the matron to the place where she had spotted him, he was nowhere to be seen. "They move about," said Mma Potokwane, sadly. "One day they live in a drain, the next day they are up a tree. There is no telling with that sort of child."

This boy was certainly not like that; he had a mother, and might even be in school. It was certainly not uncommon for children to attend school in the mornings and then work in the afternoons, especially now that the Government had made primary education compulsory. She wondered whether she would be able to speak to the mother. Botsalo Moeti had implied their relationship was a close one, but that meant very little. He would be using her, as likely as not, and she would no doubt be in awe of him—there were many such arrangements between strong men and vulnerable, desperate women. So, she thought, this woman, from her position of weakness, would not be what Clovis Andersen would call an "independent witness." *If somebody works under somebody,* the great authority wrote, *then do not expect that person to tell the truth about the person above him. He may either lie to protect his superior, lie because he is afraid of him, or lie in order to get revenge for some insult or slight.*

Mma Ramotswe decided that even if there would be no point in talking to the woman in the kitchen, it was still worth trying to seek out the boy; he knew something—she was sure of it. If he was in school, then perhaps she could speak to him there. That would involve finding the most likely village school for him to attend and then speaking to the teacher there. She would require some sort of pretext for this. Could she offer to give a talk to the school? "The Life of a Private Detective" by Mma Precious Ramotswe. They would be surprised, she thought, and might insist on her obtaining permission from the Ministry of Education or the local council or something like that. No, that would not work; it would be far better to use the tactic that she had employed on so many previous occasions when she needed something, and that was to ask for it directly. It was a rather obvious thing to do, but in her experience it was usually very effective. If you want to know the answer to something, then go and ask somebody. It was a simple but effective adage—one that perhaps should be embroidered on a sampler and sold at fundraising sales. Well, she would try it in this case, and see what happened. And if she drew a blank, then there was still another lead to follow: the key ring that had been found near the scene of the crime.

She had no idea what to make of that, but she was now getting closer to home, and she decided to concentrate on her driving and on the thought of the meal that she would shortly be preparing. There was a large chunk of fine Botswana beef waiting in the fridge, and as she turned into Zebra Drive she imagined that she could even smell it. It would gladden the heart of Mr. J.L.B. Matekoni, who loved beef, and it would be good for the children too, who loved all sorts of food, without any exception that she had yet discovered. She was of that school of thought too. Beef, pumpkin, potatoes, stringy green beans, melon—all of these things were loved by Mma Ramotswe; as were cakes, biscuits, doughnuts, and red bush tea. Life was very full.

MMA MAKUTSI also prepared a meal that evening, although she was cooking for two rather than four. Phuti had told her he would be late, as he had a meeting with a furniture supplier and would not be able to get away until almost seven o'clock. That meant that they would not sit down to eat for at least half an hour after their normal dinner-time. "Not that I mind waiting," he said over the telephone. "I'd wait for ten hours or more for your cooking, Grace. I'd wait all day."

It was a typical gallant remark by a man whose good manners stood out, even in a country noted for its politeness.

Mma Makutsi laughed. "I will not keep you waiting longer than is absolutely necessary," she said. "We shall sit down at the table the moment you come in the door."

"Yes," he said. "And then we can discuss the wedding. There are some details I must ask you about."

She hesitated. What details did he have in mind? She thought of her shoes—or, rather, the remnants of her shoes. If he asked her about those, then she would have to confess that they were already destroyed, and he might wonder why she had not spoken to him about that the previous day.

"I'd like that," she said blandly. "We have so much to plan."

Now, with the meal almost ready and the hands of the clock inching round to seven-fifteen, she took a deep breath and told herself not to worry. Phuti was a kind man, and he would understand if she told him about the shoe incident. She would tell him straightaway, she decided—the moment he came in through the door.

Shortly before seven-thirty she saw the beam of his car's headlights swing past her paw-paw tree and come to rest on her front window. The lights threw the pattern of the bars on the window against her kitchen wall, and then she heard a car door slam. The car moved off. That would be his driver going away.

She was ready for him at the door. He smiled as she asked him in. "I am very hungry now," he said.

He sat down, his injured leg sticking out at an angle that she was only now getting used to. The prosthetic ankle and foot were concealed by a sock and a shoe, but every so often the unnatural angle they adopted reminded one that they were there. He was confident that they would work well, he had said; the prosthetic appliance people had done a remarkable job. "Of course I'm lucky," he pointed out. "There are people who cannot afford a leg. They cannot work. They lose their jobs. All for a leg." He paused, then added, "That is, in places like Malawi. Not here. We are lucky."

She had said, "Yes, we are lucky." And she had meant it. Mma Makutsi's memory of poverty was a recent one, and there were members of her family who, if they were to lose a leg, would never be able to afford an artificial one, were it not for the hospitals that the country's diamonds paid for.

She invited Phuti to the table and began to serve their dinner.

"This wedding of ours," he said. "It is getting closer and closer. We must make more plans."

Mma Makutsi nodded. "I have made a list. There is one column of things for you to do and one of things for me to do."

Phuti expressed satisfaction over this approach. "But before we go into that," he said, "you must tell me what you are wearing. What about those shoes? Have you bought them yet?"

Mma Makutsi looked down at her plate. It was a direct and unambiguous question—exactly what she had most feared. Had he simply made a general enquiry about her outfit, she could have talked at length and in great detail about her dress, or about the outfit she had planned for her bridesmaid. But this was a question that would be rather difficult to avoid.

"Those shoes?" she said faintly. "It's very important to get the right shoes. You know, I was looking at a picture of a bride the other day in *Drum*. And do you know, she was wearing a pink dress and bright yellow shoes. Bright yellow shoes, Phuti! She looked ridiculous. I laughed and laughed, and so did Mma Ramotswe."

Phuti Radiphuti smiled. "Yes, very silly. She should have worn pink shoes to go with her pink dress, or maybe a yellow dress to go with her yellow shoes." He took a forkful of food and then continued, his mouth half full, "But did you buy those shoes?"

Mma Makutsi looked vaguely into the middle distance. "Shoes? Oh, those shoes. They are very nice . . . You know, I've been wondering about your suit. Should we have it dry-cleaned now and put away in one of those plastic bags, or should we—"

"It has been dry-cleaned already," said Phuti. "It is in a bag and the bag is in a cupboard. It is very safe. But what about the shoes? Did you buy them?"

Mma Makutsi put down her fork and wiped her mouth carefully on a corner of her paper table napkin. "You are a very handsome man," she said.

Phuti looked surprised. "I am just an ordinary man . . ."

"No," said Mma Makutsi. "You are one of the most handsome men in Botswana. That is what people say, you know."

Phuti smiled nervously. "I think that there are many more handsome men than me. There definitely are."

Mma Makutsi edged her chair towards his, a curious manoeuvre that involved her folding the seat of the chair as she pushed it closer to Phuti. "I'd like to kiss you, Phuti," she said.

He dropped his knife onto his plate; there was a loud clatter.

"Do not be shy," said Mma Makutsi.

"I . . . I . . ." He had not stammered for a long time, but now it came back.

Mma Makutsi inclined herself forward and planted a kiss on his cheek.

"There," she said. "I am happy now that I have kissed you."

Phuti's lower jaw seemed to quiver. "Oh," he said.

"Yes," she said. "I am very happy."

He was silent for a moment. Then he said, "With reference to that previous kiss . . ."

"Yes?"

"Would it be possible to have another one?"

Mma Makutsi reached for his hand and squeezed it. "Of course," she said. "There are lots and lots of kisses."

There was no further discussion of shoes.

AFTER THEY HAD FINISHED DINNER and Puso and Motholeli had been put to bed, Mma Ramotswe and Mr. J.L.B. Matekoni sat together out on the verandah of their house on Zebra Drive. They often did this after a meal, savouring the slightly cooler breeze that sometimes moved between the trees, listening to the sounds of the night, so different from those of the day. Insects who were silent from dawn to dusk had their say once the sun went down, knowing, perhaps, that the birds were elsewhere. Those who lived in the Kalahari, or on its fringes, were told as children that these chirruping noises at night, these sounds that were like high-pitched clicks, were the stars in the sky calling their hunting dogs. And it sounded just like that, thought Mma Ramotswe, although all those things that sound so right were often just poetry, really—the gravy we put on reality to make it taste a bit better.

It was a good time for sitting together, Mma Ramotswe felt, and it was not necessary to say anything. That evening, the sky was all but white with stars, filled with acres and acres of constellations, right down to the horizon. She had learned the names of some of these clusters when she was younger, but had forgotten most of them now, apart from the Southern Cross, which could be seen hanging over the sky towards Lobatse, a pointer to the distant Cape and its cold waters. And the Milky Way was there too—she had always been able to identify that, like a swirl of milk in an ocean of dark tea. As a girl she had imagined the Milky Way was the curtain of heaven, a notion she had been sorry to abandon as she had grown up. But she would not abandon a belief in heaven itself, wherever that might be, because she felt that if she gave that up then there would be very little left. Heaven may not turn out to be the place of her imagining, she conceded—the place envisaged in the old Botswana stories, a place inhabited by gentle white cattle, with sweet breath—but it would surely be something not too unlike that, at least in the way it felt; a place where late people would be given all that they had lacked on this earth—a place of love for those who had not been loved, a place where those who had had nothing would find they had everything the human heart could desire.

She looked at Mr. J.L.B. Matekoni, sitting beside her, a mug of tea in his hands.

"Thinking of ?" she asked. "What do they say? I'll give you a thebe if you tell me your thoughts."

He laughed. "Some of my thoughts are not worth a thebe."

"I can be the judge of that."

"Charlie," he said. "I was thinking of Charlie. And you?"

He turned to her, and for a moment there was light in his eyes, a reflection of the half-lit doorway behind them.

"Me? I was thinking of the next thing I should be thinking of. I have a case that I need to deal with."

He nodded. "That Moeti business?"

"Yes."

"I do not know that man. I could ask around, though, if you want me to. There is a man at the automotive trades school whose brother lives down there, I think. Or cousin. Or somebody."

She smiled at the thought. It was like that in Botswana—people knew one another, or if they did not, they thought they did. And that was how she wanted it. There were places, she realised, where everybody was a stranger and where, when you saw somebody, you knew that you might never see them again in this life. She could not imagine Botswana being like that. Here there were no real strangers—even if you did not know a person, he was still the brother or cousin of somebody whom you might know, or whom somebody else would know. And people did not come from nowhere, as seemed to be the case in those distant big cities; everyone had a place to which they were anchored by ties of blood, by ties of land.

"Thank you," she said. "But don't bother to speak to your friend. I have had an idea." She told him about the boy, Mpho, who surely went to the local school. Teachers, she said, were helpful as long as you treated them with sufficient respect; she would have a word with the village teacher and see what came of that.

Mr. J.L.B. Matekoni thought for a moment. "I have a cousin who is a teacher in those parts," he said. "He is not the one you want to speak to, I'm afraid, but he will know that one. His school is on the other side of the Lobatse road, but roads are—"

"Nothing," said Mma Ramotswe. "Roads go through the land, not through people."

"Exactly," said Mr. J.L.B. Matekoni. I am a mechanic, he thought, and I cannot put it as well as Mma Ramotswe can. But what she said about roads was quite true, he decided, even if he felt that the matter would require further reflection. "Shall I ask him, then?"

Mma Ramotswe nodded. "Just an introduction, Rra. Just ask

him to tell the teacher that there will be a lady coming down from Gaborone who wants to talk to him. Or her, if the teacher is a lady. Say that this lady will not want to talk for long and will be no bother at all."

He could not imagine Mma Ramotswe ever being a bother to anybody at all, and he told her so. She thanked him, and then they went on to finish their tea.

CHAPTER TEN

THE TEACHER WAS A SMALL MAN

MR. J.L.B. MATEKONI was proved right. His cousin knew the teacher at the village school close to the Moeti farm. He would send a boy, he said, to let the other teacher know that Mma Ramotswe was coming; it was only ten miles there and back—nothing for a young boy who probably walked five miles to school every day anyway. He would do so immediately, first thing that morning.

"In that case," said Mma Ramotswe to Mma Makutsi, "I shall go down there straightaway, Mma. You will be in charge here. The office is in your hands."

"I am ready for that," said Mma Makutsi, adding, "I have often thought of what would happen if you had an accident, Mma."

Mma Ramotswe, who was retrieving the key for her van from its drawer, looked up in surprise. "An accident?"

Mma Makutsi was momentarily flustered. "Heaven forbid that it should happen, Mma. I was just thinking of what would happen to the business if you were to have an accident and . . ."

"Die?"

"No, no, Mma Ramotswe. Not die. Just be in hospital for a while. I wondered what would happen here in the agency. Would I need to get an assistant? Would I be able to handle all the important cases? Those are the things that I was thinking about." She paused. "But it is like thinking of what would happen if Botswana suddenly became a very wet country, or if cattle learned Setswana, or something equally unlikely. Just dreaming, really."

Mma Ramotswe straightened up. "Well, I'm sure that you would handle everything very well," she said. "Just as I hope I would, if you were ever to have an accident, which I very much hope never happens, Mma."

Mma Makutsi changed the subject, and talked about some correspondence that had been dictated by Mma Ramotswe but still had to be sent off. She would do that, she said, and do some filing, too, if she had the time. Mma Ramotswe thanked her, and left.

SHELL: the shell of an ostrich egg. Somebody had broken it and left the fragments by the side of the path that led to the school. It was a neatly kept path, one of those Mma Ramotswe would describe as a *government path,* marked on each side by a line of whitewashed stones. In the old days of the Protectorate, when the British still had their district commissioners, there were many such paths throughout Africa, and whitewashed tree trunks too. This habit of whitewashing had lingered in some places, where people thought of it as a way of holding disorder at bay: lines of white stones represented structure, a bulwark against the encroachment of the bush.

The ostrich shell was out of place; perhaps one of the children had brought it in to show the others and had dropped it, or there had been some childish fight that had led to its destruction. Mma Ramotswe reached down and pocketed a piece, feeling the thickness of the shell as she did so. Then, she continued on her way to the small cluster of buildings—no more than two or three—that made up the local primary school.

"Yes, Mma?"

A woman had emerged from the smaller of the two buildings and was staring at Mma Ramotswe.

Mma Ramotswe began the traditional greeting. Was this woman well? Had she slept well? And the woman asked the same questions of her, and then again said, "Yes, Mma?"

"I have come to speak to the teacher," said Mma Ramotswe. "My husband knows the teacher at the other school—the one over on that side. He is his cousin, and he said—"

The woman raised a hand to stop her. "Yes, you are that lady, Mma. We have heard that you would be coming. There was a message. You are welcome."

"Thank you. I will not take much of the teacher's time."

The woman indicated that this did not matter. "I am the school secretary. There is just me and the teacher. We are the staff, and we get very few visitors, Mma. We are very happy that you've come to see us."

Mma Ramotswe followed the woman into what she saw was a small office. The walls were plastered, but unpainted. There were no ceiling boards, just a criss-cross of wooden beams and the underside of a corrugated-iron roof above. In the centre of the room there stood a rectangular, three-drawered desk of the sort found in a thousand government offices up and down the country. Behind it there was a revolving chair covered in threadbare, greasy brown fabric. At the side of the room, pushed up against the wall, was another, smaller desk on which an unstable tower of box files had been built.

"This is the teacher's desk," said the secretary, pointing to the desk in the middle of the room. "And that one over there is mine. This is also the staff room." She smiled at her own joke. "When teachers come from bigger schools, they say, 'Where is your staff room?' And I say, 'You are in it right now!' "

She gestured to a spare chair that had been placed in front of the teacher's desk and invited Mma Ramotswe to sit down. "You sit there and I shall fetch the teacher."

While the secretary was out of the room, Mma Ramotswe looked about her. The walls were almost bare, apart from a small cluster of notices pinned to a square of discoloured soft board. There was a timetable of the hours from eight in the morning until one in the afternoon, with a subject noted after each: eight—roll-call and arithmetic; nine—Setswana and geography of Botswana; and so on through the day. Reading it brought a smile to Mma Ramotswe's face, as did a small notice addressed to "All Staff," setting out the dates of the school terms. It would be like putting up notices to herself and Mma Makutsi, she thought, although she could include notices about tea and the washing of teacups addressed to Mr. J.L.B. Matekoni and the apprentices.

A voice came from behind her: "Mma?"

She spun round. The teacher was standing in the doorway, the secretary behind him. She drew in her breath sharply; she had not expected this. The teacher was very short—a dwarf, in fact—and the secretary, who was a woman of barely average height, towered over him.

She recovered her poise quickly. "*Dumela,* Rra. I was just looking at the timetable. You must be very busy."

The teacher inclined his head. "There is just me," he said. "Me and this lady here, who you have already met."

He crossed the floor and extended a hand in greeting. Mma Ramotswe reached down; it seemed so strange to be bending to shake hands with a man. His handshake felt firm, almost too firm, as he gripped her.

"Please sit in that chair, Mma," he said. "I will go to my desk."

He walked round the desk, his head barely showing above its surface. "My name is Oreeditse Modise. And you, Mma, are . . . ?"

She gave her name, and he wrote it down solemnly on a pad of paper on his desk. That done, he looked up at her and smiled. There was something about the smile that touched her; it was as if he were reaching out to her.

"I am married to Mr. J.L.B. Matekoni," she said. "He is the cousin of your colleague at the other school."

Mr. Modise made a further note. "Cousin," he said. "That is very good."

"I am a detective," said Mma Ramotswe.

She expected him to note this down too, but he did not. This information had clearly surprised him, and he threw a glance in the direction of his secretary, who opened her mouth slightly in a silent *oh*.

"Not a police detective," said Mma Ramotswe quickly. "I am a person who works for people who have private problems. That sort of detective."

She saw him relax.

"Oh," he said. "I see."

"There has been a very unpleasant incident at a farm near here," she said. "There was—"

"I know all about that, Mma." Mr. Modise put down his pencil and leaned back in his chair. "There was a dastardly attack on some innocent cows over at Mr. Moeti's place. Very bad."

The secretary let out a wail. "Very bad! Cows! Cows!"

"So you're working on that, are you, Mma? Then I am very happy to assist in any way. We cannot have people attacking cattle in this country. We cannot."

"No, no!" shrieked the secretary.

Mma Ramotswe felt that the temperature in the room was rising rather higher than perhaps it should. "We must remain calm," she said quietly. "It is the sort of thing that makes anybody angry. But we must remain calm if we are to deal with this."

"Yes, indeed," said Mr. Modise, glancing at the secretary. "I am calm now. You need not worry, Mma. We are all calm."

Mma Ramotswe realised that her fears as to their cooperation were misplaced: these two, at least, were allies—the entire staff. She told them why she had come to see them. There was a boy called Mpho, whose mother worked in the Moeti house . . .

"Mpho?" said the teacher. "That boy is one of ours. He is in the classroom. He is there right now." He picked up his pencil and wrote the name on his pad of paper: MPHO, in capital letters.

Mma Ramotswe clasped her hands together involuntarily. It had worked.

"Does that boy know something?" asked Mr. Modise.

She explained about her meeting with the child on the Moeti farm. "I am sure that he knows what happened," she said. "But I am equally sure that he was frightened. So I need to speak to him."

"Yes, yes," said the teacher, making a signal to his secretary. "Fetch him straightaway. Then we can ask him about this thing. We shall get the truth out of him and he will tell us, or we shall give him a beating."

Mma Ramotswe gasped. "Please! Let's not beat anybody. And . . ." She paused. It would be impossible to speak to the boy in the teacher's presence, and yet she would need to be tactful. "If you wouldn't mind too much, I think it might be better for me to speak to him privately, Rra."

"Why? I am his teacher."

"Yes, and I'm sure that he respects you very much. But in my experience, Rra—and I have been a detective for a few years now—I find that some witnesses, and particularly children, do not speak freely if there is somebody they like and respect in the room. They say what they think that person will want them to say, Rra. It is very curious, but human nature is strange, and that is what I think."

He looked at her doubtfully for a moment, and then nodded his agreement. "You're the expert, Mma."

She thanked him for his understanding, and noticed how he beamed at the compliment. What compliments were paid to a teacher out in the bush, she wondered; and to a teacher like this, a small man who must be accustomed to the stares of others?

"It is nothing, Mma," he said. "Nothing at all. Would you like to speak to him in here, or outside?"

"Outside," she said quickly.

THE BOY MPHO, part-time herd boy, son of a domestic servant, a rather puny little boy who probably did not know who his father was—a boy with a running nose discharging mucus onto his upper lip—stood before her, shaking with fear.

They were under a tree a short distance from the schoolroom itself. It was hot, and the shade was welcome. From inside, through the open windows of the schoolroom, came the sound of the children reciting their tables. *Two fours make eight; three fours make twelve; four fours . . .*

"You remember me, Mpho?"

He looked up at her briefly, and then down at his feet. He was barefoot, and his feet were dusty. Such little toes, thought Mma Ramotswe.

"Yes, Mma. Yes."

She smiled at him. "You mustn't be afraid of me, Mpho. Look . . . look here." She reached into her pocket and took out the fragment of eggshell.

He glanced at the shell and said, "It's broken."

Mma Ramotswe handed it to him. "You can have it, if you like. There. Some people think that this brings good luck. Have you heard that before?"

He shook his head as he reached out to take the shell from her. She saw that he used both hands to receive the gift, as was proper. Somebody was still teaching children the right thing to do, even a poor little boy like this who could not have had much in his short life. She wondered whether he had ever been taken to Gaborone—probably not; or given a treat—almost certainly not. She remembered her first ice cream and the pleasure she had derived from that; how lucky she felt to have had a childhood in which she had been able to lay down good memories.

"When I saw you last time, Mpho," she said gently, "I thought you were a little bit frightened of something. I don't want you to be frightened now."

He continued to stare down at the ground. He was still shaking, she noticed.

"Sometimes, you know," she continued, "it's better to talk about something rather than to keep it inside you. Nobody is going to punish you for speaking to me, you see. And I won't tell anybody that you have spoken to me. I promise you that."

He remained silent. A shadow crossed the ground beside them, the shadow of a large bird, a buzzard perhaps, that was soaring between them and the sun.

"Rra Moeti won't know," she said quietly.

The effect of this was immediate. He looked up sharply, into her eyes; and she saw his fear.

"He cannot harm you," she said. "He is not allowed to harm you. There is . . ." What, she wondered, was there to stop Mr. Moeti harming this child? The law? As embodied by whom? A policeman in a police post fifteen miles away? An official in an office in Gaborone even further removed from the world inhabited by this boy? "It is not allowed," she said.

He stared at her. His lip was quivering, and then the tears came. She stepped forward and put her arms around the boy as he sobbed. She felt him shaking in her embrace, the shoulders so narrow, so vulnerable.

She did not say anything until his sobs had subsided and she was applying her handkerchief to his nose. "There, Mpho. That's better now."

"I'm sorry," he stuttered. "I'm sorry I did it, Mma. I'm very bad and they can send me to prison now."

Mma Ramotswe had not expected this. "You . . . you did it, Mpho? Those cattle? The cattle you looked after?"

He nodded silently.

"But why? Why would you harm the cattle?"

"Because Rra Moeti is a bad man, Mma. He has done bad things to my mother."

Mma Ramotswe drew in her breath. The inexplicable becomes explicable, she thought. Yes, it was more or less as she had imagined. The poor servant woman and the powerful farmer. It was nothing new; it would be happening up and down the country—up and down every country, no matter where it was. People with money and land treated those without either of those things as they wished. Poor people were at their mercy; it had always been like this, and, sadly, it would probably not ever change very much. Oh, there would be changes on the surface, with laws and regulations making it harder for people to take advantage of others, but there would always be places, places off the beaten track, that laws and regulations never reached. And there would always be men of the view that laws that protected women had nothing to do with them, or were not meant to be taken seriously.

She took stock of the situation. The boy must have seen his mother abused—beaten, perhaps, or made to cower—and decided to take matters into his own hands. He must have felt completely powerless in the face of his mother's tormentor, and then realised that there was a way in which he could strike back at Moeti. Every

Motswana loved his cattle, and Mr. Moeti was no exception. If one really wanted to hurt him, then what would be easier than to take a knife to the very cattle who knew and trusted one?

She was not sure what to say. Mpho had caused major loss and she could hardly ignore that, especially as it was her responsibility to find out what had happened. But how could she throw him on the mercy of Mr. Moeti—the very man who had been cruel to his mother? She remembered, too, that she had promised him that Mr. Moeti would never know that he had spoken to her.

She looked down at the boy. "Listen to me, Mpho. What you did was terrible—one of the worst things anybody can do. You must never do anything like that again, Mpho. Never. Do you understand?"

"You are going to beat me, Mma?"

She tried not to smile. "Of course not. What I'm saying is this: I can see how you felt very angry when you saw your mother being harmed. But you can't go and do something like that, even if you think that man deserved it. It is not the way we do things here in Botswana. Do you understand?"

He had stopped shaking, she noticed, and she thought that his voice sounded stronger.

"I understand, Mma."

She looked at him. She suspected that this boy knew all about punishment, and children who knew about punishment often did not need to learn any more.

"All right," she said. "You remember what I said. You remember it. Now, let's go back to the classroom."

She walked him back to the schoolroom, her hand in his. As they crossed the short expanse of hot red earth she asked him whether he enjoyed being at the school. "And Mr. Modise?" she said. "Do you like your teacher?"

Mpho nodded. "I like him, Mma, even if he is too small, Mma."

"Yes, he is small," she said. "But you must always remember: small people are often big inside—and that is what matters."

"Maybe," muttered Mpho.

SHE DROVE BACK to Gaborone deep in thought. There were some enquiries that fizzled out remarkably quickly, when a well-placed question led to the rapid unravelling of what had seemed to be a tangled and opaque skein of confusing facts and half-truths. She had not expected the solution in this case to come quite so quickly, and so simply; but that, she reminded herself, was how many problems in this life sorted themselves out—quickly and simply.

She found herself thinking of Mpho's mother—the woman she had met in the Moeti house; of her subservient manner in the presence of her employer; of his dismissive manner towards her. She wished that she could do something about that—could release the woman in some way from the near-servitude in which she must live her life. But what could she do? This sort of oppression was nothing new; men did that to women everywhere, all the time, and there were some cases, less common perhaps, where women did it to men. Things had become better, of course, with the achievement by women of greater equality, but the news of all that would hardly have penetrated out there. A farm could be a little world, a law unto itself; even a house could be that too.

And then she thought of the boy. Her first reaction had been to believe him. His distress had clearly been genuine, and the words of his confession had come tumbling out unrehearsed. But children made things up, including confessions.

For the time being, though, she would act on the assumption that he had been telling the truth. One thing was clear: the confession did not put the matter to rest. She had her duty to Mr. Moeti to consider; she might not like him, but he was, after all, her client, and she could hardly keep the truth from him. At the same time she realised that she could not go to him and reveal that Mpho was responsible for the attack. Not only was there her promise to the boy, but if she did identify him as having been responsible for the incident, then she would be accountable for whatever harm came to him, or indeed to his mother. Could she tell Mr. Moeti that she had discovered the culprit but that she would punish him herself? Mr. Moeti would hardly accept that, and he would have a point.

When she arrived back at the office, while Mma Makutsi made tea, Mma Ramotswe gave her an account of her visit to the school. She told her assistant about Mr. Modise, which interested Mma Makutsi a great deal; she had a cousin who was very short, she said, and had fallen into an anteater's burrow. "He was too short to get out," she explained. "And so he had to stay there until somebody came that way and pulled him out. But before that the anteater came back and was very cross that there was this short person in his burrow. Apparently he growled and tried to bite my cousin. It was a very dangerous situation."

Mma Makutsi had several more stories to tell about this cousin, but Mma Ramotswe gently interrupted her after the second story—a rather long-winded and unfortunate tale about the cousin's marriage to an unusually tall young woman. "Perhaps you could tell me the rest of the story some other time, Mma," she said. "I need to talk to you about this Moeti business."

"But it was very funny," persisted Mma Makutsi. "You see, when a very short man marries a tall woman—"

"I can imagine," said Mma Ramotswe. "But I really have to make some sort of decision, Mma, and it would be helpful if you could advise me."

Mma Makutsi put aside thoughts of short men and tall women and gave Mma Ramotswe her attention. She listened intently as Mma Ramotswe described the boy's sudden confession, clicking her tongue in disapproval. "Children do very bad things these days," she said, "because they see television. If you turn on the television, what do you see, Mma? You see people being violent—that is all that there is. And if you were a child watching that, what would you think? You'd think that this is how we should behave—breaking things, breaking people."

Mma Ramotswe understood that, but she wondered whether it applied in this case. "I doubt if that boy sees television," she said. "He is a herd boy and his mother is a kitchen servant, second-class. I doubt if he has seen television."

"Then he will have heard about these things, Mma. That is how it happens. And remember that all those violent television signals are all around us, in the air. How do you know that violence doesn't spread that way?"

Mma Ramotswe did not wish to argue about this novel, and in her view highly dubious, theory. What she wanted to find out was what Mma Makutsi would *do* about this. "But what would you do, Mma?" she pressed.

Mma Makutsi thought for a moment. "I would tell Moeti that you have heard that he has brought this upon himself by behaving badly. Then I would tell him that it was unlikely to happen again. If you have stopped it, then I think that you have done him a good service."

Mma Ramotswe was doubtful. "I don't know if he'll look on it that way," she said.

"Well I don't see how it would help him to punish that boy," said Mma Makutsi.

"You're right," said Mma Ramotswe.

"You could go to the police," said Mma Makutsi. "The police are always there."

Mma Ramotswe sighed. "I promised the boy that I wouldn't speak to anybody about what he said. Perhaps I shouldn't have made that promise, but I did. At that point I was thinking of him as a witness, you see, not as the person who did it."

"But, why didn't Moeti go to the police himself?" asked Mma Makutsi. "It's up to him if he wants to make it a police matter. He didn't—he came to you. So in fact it is not for you to go to the police, Mma. No."

"Perhaps not," said Mma Ramotswe.

"Well then," said Mma Makutsi, in a certain tone of satisfaction. "Well then, that solves that, doesn't it? QED—as we were taught to say at the Botswana Secretarial College."

"QED?" asked Mma Ramotswe. "What does that stand for?"

Mma Makutsi looked uncomfortable. "QED? I'm not one hundred per cent sure. I think it might mean *There you are,* or maybe *I told you so . . .*"

Mma Ramotswe came to her rescue; she understood Mma Makutsi's sensitivity, and she did not want to show her up. "You may not be one hundred per cent sure," she said. "But I imagine that you'll be at least ninety-seven per cent sure!"

It was a very good joke, and it enabled them both to leave the issue of the Moeti attack and start thinking of something else. But Mma Ramotswe remained less than satisfied. She felt vaguely guilty, as if she had embarked upon a plan to conceal a major crime. And that, she suddenly realised, was what she had almost done; it was not for her to decide whether or not to disclose what had happened. A crime had been committed, even if it was a crime by a child—something that should normally be dealt with by a stern talking-to and promises by parents. No, she would have to go and see the boy's mother and hand the affair over to her. She would plead for the boy, but she could not protect him, nor his mother, completely; the world was not as she would like it to be, but there was very little she could do to change that. Withholding the truth from Mr. Moeti was wrong, but it was also wrong to break a promise to a small, vulnerable child, who would never forget that an adult he trusted had let him down. So here she was faced with two evils, and the lesser one, she was sure, was unquestionably the one to choose.

CHAPTER ELEVEN

CHARLIE COMES TO ZEBRA DRIVE, BY NIGHT

THAT EVENING Charlie came to the house on Zebra Drive. He came quietly, appearing at the back door like a wraith, startling Mma Ramotswe, who was washing up after dinner. She had been standing at the sink, her hands immersed in soapy water, when she noticed the movement outside, half in the darkness, half in the square of light thrown out from the window.

"Charlie!"

He did not hear her; he was staring in through the window now, as if searching the room. She waved a hand, signalling to him, and he glanced at her.

"I'll let you in," she mouthed.

He did not look as if he wanted to come in, as he now seemed to retreat back into the shadows.

"Wait. Don't go away."

She dried her hands perfunctorily before opening the door that led from the kitchen to the yard outside. The open door cast an oblong of light in the yard outside, revealing the figure of Charlie, standing awkwardly by one of the struggling shrubs that Mma

Ramotswe had planted in that difficult, rather sandy part of her garden.

She made an effort to appear natural, as if the arrival by night of an unannounced visitor lurking in the darkness was nothing unusual.

"So, Fanwell passed on my message," she said. "I'm glad that you've come."

He mumbled something that she did not catch.

"Why don't you come into the kitchen?" she asked. "I can give you something to eat, if you like."

He shook his head. "I'm not hungry. And I don't want to see the boss."

She made a gesture of acceptance. "You don't have to see him. We can talk out here." She moved towards him, taking his hand. "I often like to come out into the garden at night, you know. It's a good time to smell the plants. They smell different at night, you see. They—"

"I cannot stay long," he said.

"You don't have to. You can go any time. But it would be better, don't you think, to talk about this."

She drew him towards the side of the house, to two old iron chairs they kept outside and rarely sat in, but he resisted.

"It is my business," he said sullenly. "I am not a child."

She squeezed his hand. "Of course it's your business, Charlie. Of course it is."

"Then why does she shout at me, that woman? Why does she—"

"Mma Makutsi?"

He sniffed. "She is like a cow. She is always talking like a cow."

Mma Ramotswe shook her head. "You two don't see eye to eye, do you?" It was, she felt, putting it mildly; Mma Makutsi and Charlie had sparred for as long as they had known each other—a personality thing, Mr. J.L.B. Matekoni had said. Petrol and diesel, he had added; they don't mix.

"She cannot tell me what to do," continued Charlie. "Those babies . . ."

Mma Ramotswe waited for him to finish the sentence, but he fell silent. "Those babies," she said gently. "Your children."

"I did not tell her to have them," he said. "It is her fault. She is a stupid girl."

Mma Ramotswe bit her lip. Mma Makutsi, she felt, might have a point; she kept her voice from rising. "Nobody has to marry somebody they don't want to marry," she said evenly. "It is not a good idea to make people do that—they will only feel unhappy."

"I don't want to get married yet," said Charlie.

"Then don't," said Mma Ramotswe. "And she may not want you to, anyway. Have you spoken to her about it?"

He had not, he said. He had not seen Prudence since she had told him that she was pregnant.

Mma Ramotswe was still trying to be gentle, but her question slipped out. "Why? Why did you do something like that, Charlie?"

She saw the effect of her question: there was pain in his expression; she could see that, even in the faint light from the window.

"What could I do, Mma? I cannot look after her children."

"*Your* children, Charlie."

He opened his mouth to say something, but she stopped him. "But let's not speak about that, Charlie. Would you like me to talk to her?"

She saw his eyes open wide.

"You, Mma?"

She sighed. "Yes, Charlie. I can go. Sometimes it is easier if you get somebody to talk to somebody else for you. They can explain.

They can tell the other person how you're feeling. That makes it easier."

She could tell that he was torn, and she pressed her advantage. "I could tell her that you feel you can't get married, but that you would like to do something—even if it is not very much—to help with the babies. It's not money, I think—not in this case. It's maybe just enough for you to visit the babies so that as they grow up they have a father."

He was listening, she thought.

"But what if she makes me marry her?"

"I don't think she will. And I can tell her not to talk about that—if she'll listen to me."

Charlie was silent. "And Mma Makutsi?"

Mma Ramotswe did not hesitate. "I'll talk to her too. I don't think she will say anything." She hesitated. "Remember, I am her boss, after all. And I know that she can be a bit . . . a bit forceful at times."

She had not anticipated it, but this remark seemed to change everything.

"You can tell her to shut up, Mma?" Charlie said. "That is very good. All the time I thought that everyone agreed with her. There were all these women. You. Her. Mma Potokwane too. All against me."

"Well, I'm not against you, Charlie. I promise you that." She paused. "And you'll come back to work tomorrow? If you do, I'll tell Mr. J.L.B. Matekoni. He won't say anything."

"Nothing?"

"I'll talk to him too. He'll understand."

Charlie considered this. "He's a good man."

"Of course he is, Charlie, and so are you, you know."

Had it not been quite so dark, Mma Ramotswe would have seen the effect of her words. Charlie, who had been slouching, as if expecting some sort of physical blow, seemed to grow in stature. The furtiveness with which he had acted disappeared, and he stepped forward, as if putting the shadows, real and otherwise, behind him. "Thank you, Mma. Thank you . . ." His voice became choked.

She looked at her watch. "It's getting late, Charlie. Would you like me to run you home in my van?"

"I am at Fanwell's place."

"I can take you there. Go to the van. I'll fetch the key."

They drove across town to Old Naledi, where Fanwell lived with his grandmother. It was a poor neighbourhood—the poorest in town—and the lighting was non-existent. At one point they took a wrong turning and drove up an unfamiliar road. Charlie thought that they would be able to get back to where they wanted to be if they took the next road on the right, and told Mma Ramotswe to continue.

"You could get really lost in here," she said. "Even in daytime."

"There are too many houses," said Charlie. "They shouldn't let people put these things up." He peered into the night. "Turn here, Mma. This road goes round the back there."

Mma Ramotswe swung the wheel of the van. The beam of the headlights moved across a makeshift fence and the walls of a house behind it, then back to illuminate the surface of a road that was not much more than an urban track, unpaved and bumpy. A struggling tree beside it and then a gate, another house, a bit larger this one and painted an indeterminate colour—in that light it was difficult to make out just what—and on the edge of the road a bit further along, half on the track, half off, parked carelessly as every vehicle seemed to be in this ramshackle place, a small van, and in this case there was no mistaking its colour, which was white.

She saw it a few seconds before Charlie did, and put her foot firmly on the brake.

"No," he said. "This is the right way. Carry on."

"Charlie," she stuttered.

And then he saw it too. "Oh," he said. "That looks like your old van, Mma."

Mma Ramotswe engaged gear and drove forward slowly, stopping just short of the other van. In the glare of the headlights, the white was bright, almost shiny. She switched off the engine, but left the lights on.

"It's my van, Charlie. I know it."

"There are many such vans, Mma. White is a popular colour."

"This one is mine," she said. "I'm going to check. There is a place where a post hit me."

She got out of the van and was followed by Charlie. Bending down, floodlit in the darkness, she examined the place on the bodywork where she had encountered the errant post. It was there, in exactly the right place. She straightened up and moved towards the front, peering in the window on the driver's side. Yes. It was there—the large scratch on the metal dashboard that Puso as a small boy had made with a knitting needle.

She turned to Charlie. The lights were shining directly into her eyes, two great suns in the darkness, and she could not make out his face. "It is definitely my van, Charlie. There is that dent, and the scratch that Puso made. This is my tiny white van."

He had been persuaded. "Well," he said, touching the bodywork affectionately. "So here it is, Mma. Our old friend. Still going."

She looked about her. The house outside which the van was parked was slightly better than many around it—there was a well-kept yard with a small chicken coop, a lean-to latrine with a tap on the outer wall, a path on the side of which small stones had been lined. The house itself was in darkness, although lights were on in neighbouring homes.

"So, Mma," said Charlie. "It is good to see this van still going. It must have cost a bit to fix up. Or maybe it was done by somebody with a lot of time on his hands."

"Like me."

They both spun round. The voice had come from behind them, from the roadside rather than the yard. A man was standing in the middle of the road, a shape in the darkness.

"That is my van," he said, addressing himself to Charlie. "What are you doing, Rra? Why are you looking at my van?"

Mma Ramotswe answered. "We are not doing anything wrong, Rra," she said. "I used to own this van. We were driving past and I saw it. That is all."

The man came closer; now they could see him properly in the headlights. He was of stocky build, somewhere in his thirties, wearing neat khaki trousers and a white shirt. As he looked at them, they saw him relax.

"I put some work into it," he said. "But most of it was done by the man up north who bought it before me. He didn't have the time to finish, and so I did the rest."

"You are a mechanic, Rra?" asked Charlie.

"No," said the man. "I am not a mechanic. Not a proper one."

"I am," said Charlie. "Tlokweng Road Speedy Motors."

"I know the place," said the man. "That woman detective place."

"And that is me," said Mma Ramotswe. "I am that woman."

The man nodded at her. "You drove the van, Mma?"

She reached out to touch it. "For many years, Rra. Many years."

"And now? Now this nice new vehicle here?" He gestured towards the blue van. "Lucky you."

Mma Ramotswe agreed that the new van was comfortable, indeed smart. But she still loved the old van, she confessed. It had been a friend.

"I know what you mean," said the man. "You get used to a car, I think. It is like an old pair of shoes."

"It grows to fit you," said Mma Ramotswe.

The man nodded. "Well . . ."

Mma Ramotswe drew in her breath. There were moments in life when something had to be said, or be left unsaid forever. It was ridiculous—she knew it was—but she had to speak.

"Tell me, Rra, would you consider selling this van if you were given a good price—and I mean a *really* good price?"

Charlie glanced at her and frowned. She touched him on the wrist—a gesture to tell him to leave it to her.

"A really good price?"

"Yes, Rra. What if somebody paid you enough for you to buy a newer van? Not a really new one, of course, but one that had much less mileage. Much less."

The man did not hesitate. "I would say yes," he said. "Anybody with any sense would say yes if such a person came along."

"I am that person," said Mma Ramotswe quietly.

Charlie tried to intervene. "Mma, what would Mr. J.L.B. Matekoni say?"

Mma Ramotswe answered curtly. "It is my money, Charlie. Mine. And if I wish to spend it on a van, then—"

"All right," said Charlie. "But let me ask what has been done to the van."

Mma Ramotswe turned to the man. "You have already answered that, Rra, haven't you?"

The man now appeared to scent an opportunity. "Everything has been done, Mma! Everything. New this, new that, new the other thing. Yes, everything."

"There," said Mma Ramotswe to Charlie. "You heard him."

Charlie shook his head. "What is a *this*? What is a *that*? Those are not mechanical terms, Mma."

The man defended himself. "She is a lady, Rra. You do not want to burden ladies with talk about big-ends and rebores. You should know that—as a mechanic."

"That is right," said Mma Ramotswe. "There is no point in making ladies unhappy with mechanical details." She touched the car again. "Can we talk tomorrow, Rra?"

The man nodded eagerly. "I work at that electrical store at Riverwalk. You know the one?"

"I do," said Mma Ramotswe. "Can I come to see you some time soon to discuss the price?"

"Yes," agreed the man. "When you get there, you ask for Daniel. That is me. I am not always in the front, and they may have to fetch me from the back office. I am assistant manager, you see."

"Then that is what I shall do, Daniel," said Mma Ramotswe.

They said goodnight and returned to the blue van. As they drove away, Daniel waved cheerfully before opening his gate and disappearing up the path lined with stones.

"I do not think this is a good idea, Mma," said Charlie. "This van is very good. It was very expensive. What are you going to do?"

"I am going to sell it, Charlie."

He whistled. "You can't. You can't sell this good van and buy back your old van. You can't do that sort of thing, Mma."

"Can't I?" said Mma Ramotswe. "Why not? Can you tell me why not?"

SHE DROPPED CHARLIE at Fanwell's house, which was in darkness. He had become silent again, but she did not have the impression that he had changed his mind about returning. She took his hand briefly before he got out of the car and squeezed it. "You can sleep well tonight, Charlie," she said. "No need to worry."

On the way back home, she thought about what she had done. She had acted impulsively—she recognised that—but there were times when that was what you had to do. And did it matter, did it really matter that she would probably lose money in the sale of this blue van? Mr. J.L.B. Matekoni had bought it for her, but he had used the money in their joint bank account to do so, and she had put that money there from the profits of the No. 1 Ladies' Detective Agency. She and Mr. J.L.B. Matekoni shared everything and normally did not even think about who earned what, but if he were to call her to account for the sale of the blue van, she could always point out that she had effectively paid for it.

Would he understand why she felt she had to have her tiny white van back? She did not think that he would: men didn't love things in the same way as women did. They were fond of some things, of course, but she did not think that they *loved* things in that way. The heart of a man was different—every woman knew that.

That was what she thought, but then, as she drove round the roundabout near the Anglican cathedral she thought of her father, the late Obed Ramotswe, and of how he had loved his battered old hat. That was where it came from, perhaps—her love of the white van was love of exactly the same sort that her father had had for his hat. So maybe she was wrong about men; maybe they did love things in the same way as women; maybe they had just as many tears to shed for the things they had lost.

She arrived back at the house to find Mr. J.L.B. Matekoni waiting anxiously in the kitchen.

"Where have you been, Mma? I was worried."

She put the van key down on the table. "Charlie," she said. "He came to see me."

He looked incredulous. "Charlie?"

She told him of her encounter with the young man, and about his promise to return to work. "Just pretend that nothing has happened," she said. "Don't say anything. Just carry on as normal."

"But it has happened," he said.

"Yes, but there are times when something that has happened has to be treated as if it hasn't. This is one of those times, I think."

He shrugged. "I do not always understand you, Mma Ramotswe."

She laughed. "And another thing, Rra. What would you do if I did something that you thought was a very bad idea, but that I really wanted to do? What if that thing was a thing that made me very happy, but looked ridiculous to you?"

He frowned. "Something your heart was set on?"

"Yes," she said. "Something that my heart said I just had to do."

"In that case, I would say to myself: It is an odd thing that Mma Ramotswe has done, but if that is what makes her happy, then I am happy too."

She looked at him fondly; that he had been sent to her, when there were so many other, lesser men who might have been sent, was a source of constant gratitude. That we have the people we have in this life, rather than others, is miraculous, she thought; a miraculous gift.

CHAPTER TWELVE

CARBOLIC SOAP AND LIES

THE NEXT FEW DAYS were marked by the fact that virtually nothing happened. Such spells in otherwise busy lives are like breaks in bad weather: we know that they will not last, and our knowledge of their impermanence makes them seem all the more precious. But although throughout this time scarcely a soul crossed the threshold of the No. 1 Ladies' Detective Agency, both Mma Makutsi and Mma Ramotswe had more than enough to occupy their thoughts. For Mma Makutsi, the main concern was her impending wedding; the date was fast approaching, and the invitations had already been posted. Her long list of preparations was now marked by rows of ticks as task after task was completed with all the efficiency one would expect of one who, after all, had achieved a hitherto unheard-of ninety-seven per cent in her final examinations. But there were still things to do, and things to worry about, or to worry that Phuti was not worrying about enough.

An example of the latter was the cattle that would be used for the wedding feast. A very large cow and three well-fed goats had been identified for this purpose, and Phuti was meant to have arranged for them to be brought in from his family's cattle post.

Had this been done? And what about the cow he had promised her people for their feast up in Bobonong? Was this going to be purchased up there, or would it be taken up from the Radiphuti cattle post? These were important questions, and Mma Makutsi was not entirely satisfied that Phuti was on top of them. It was all very well for men; they assumed that weddings *happened,* and they often enjoyed themselves conspicuously at such events, but did they know *how* these things went off smoothly? Did men make lists, she wondered; and concluded that they did not. She had never seen a man with a list—not once—although she often saw men in the supermarket struggling to read the lists made for them by their wives. Mma Makutsi had, in fact, once helped such a man to interpret his wife's instructions and had ended up doing his entire shopping for him, consequently making herself late for an appointment at the hair-braiding salon.

While Mma Makutsi sat at her desk and thought about the wedding, Mma Ramotswe sat in her place, her mind filled with thoughts of a rather different nature. She had more than enough on her plate, she reflected, and several things that were concerning her seemed to be without obvious and immediate solution. There was Charlie, of course. He had returned to work and appeared to be coping; Mr. J.L.B. Matekoni had been tact itself, and had not even docked his wages for the missing days. But there was still the issue of Prudence, and the visit that Mma Ramotswe had promised to pay to the wronged young woman. Charlie, she suspected, had assumed that a few words to Prudence from her would solve the whole issue; they would not, thought Mma Ramotswe. He would have to make some effort, and she was not sure whether he had the staying power for that. Time would tell, as Mma Potokwane sometimes said; *time will tell, Mma Ramotswe.* Yes, Mma Potokwane, but what if time tells us what we don't want to hear?

At least with the Charlie affair she knew what she had to do. It was not that simple when she turned her attention to the other difficult problem with which she was confronted—the Moeti case. Her heart sank even as she started once again to think about it. She had decided that she could not let Mpho's deeds go unreported, but she remained deeply concerned about the small boy's safety if Mr. Moeti were to hear, even indirectly, that he was responsible for the attack on his cattle. Terrible things happened out in the country, and a person like Moeti would, as likely as not, take a sjambok to the errant herd boy. Sjamboks, those cruel cattle-hide whips, would do real damage to a small boy; she could not allow that. But how could she deal with the problem and yet keep it from Mr. Moeti? The obvious thing to do would be to speak to the boy's mother and ask her to do something about disciplining or watching the boy. But could she be sure that the information would not somehow leak out? People talked. If she went to the police and told them what had happened, they would be bound to let Mr. Moeti know who was responsible for the outrage; that was how the police operated. They had their rules, of course—it was not their fault—and one of those rules would probably state that the owner of damaged property had to be informed of who had done the damage if that fact were to emerge. Well, it had emerged—if, of course, Mpho were to be believed.

And then there was the van. That at least had been a positive development, but she had done nothing about going to see Daniel because that would involve negotiations and she was in no mood for negotiations at present. So the only thing to do, she decided, was to wait at her desk and see if anything happened. Which it did—not that day, nor the next, but the day afterwards, when everything seemed to happen at once, as is often the case.

"There is a man parking his car under the tree," said Mma

Makutsi. From her vantage point on the other side of the room, she could see through the window that Mma Ramotswe could not really look through unless she craned her neck uncomfortably.

"Coming to see us?" asked Mma Ramotswe.

"I think so. If he was going to the garage I think he would have parked his car there rather than under the tree. That is what I think, Mma." There was a note of reproach in Mma Makutsi's voice, almost as if she was suggesting that Mma Ramotswe's powers of deduction were failing. Mma Ramotswe just smiled; brides-to-be could be testy—that was a well-known fact.

Mma Ramotswe rose to her feet. "Perhaps we have a new client, Mma," she said. "And about time, I think."

"Or an old one come in to see you," said Mma Makutsi. "That is equally possible, don't you think, Mma?"

Again, Mma Ramotswe said nothing. Mma Makutsi had a lot on her mind, and once she was married these comments would surely stop.

She opened the door and saw Mr. Moeti speaking to Mr. J.L.B. Matekoni, who was directing him to the office door.

"Moeti," she whispered to Mma Makutsi. "This is him."

Mma Makutsi glanced out of the door. "I shall put on the kettle, Mma," she said. "And I am right here if you need me."

Moeti approached, holding out his hand in greeting. "So this is your place, Mma Ramotswe. It is a very nice office, I think. And very handy for that garage, too, if your car breaks down."

Mma Ramotswe smiled. "That mechanic is my husband, Rra."

"Very good," said Mr. Moeti. "And this lady is your secretary?"

"Associate detective," corrected Mma Makutsi.

Mr. Moeti made a show of apologising. "Oh, very sorry, Mma. Big mistake on my part. Very sorry."

"That is all right," said Mma Makutsi primly. "There are two detectives here. Mma Ramotswe, who is the proprietor, and myself. Would you like some tea, Rra? These mornings are so hot these days, aren't they?"

Mr. Moeti looked about the room. "Tea would be very nice, Mma. Three spoons of sugar, please." He turned to Mma Ramotswe, who was offering him the client's chair. "Yes, a very good office, Mma."

Mma Ramotswe acknowledged the compliment. She had been surprised by Mr. Moeti's appearance, and a little concerned. He would ask her for a progress report, no doubt, and that would be tricky, as she would be unable to reveal what had happened. So she would have to watch her words carefully, weighing each one to ensure that she told him nothing without telling any outright lies. *Never, ever lie to your client,* Clovis Andersen had written. *That's Rule No. 3, right up there with Rules 1 and 2. Don't lie.*

As she sat down at her desk and faced her client, the thought occurred to her that something about Mr. Moeti's visit was not quite right. When he had first contacted her, he had been careful to arrange a meeting elsewhere, wanting to avoid being seen coming to the detective agency. He had appeared frightened, and jumpy in his manner. Now, by contrast, he seemed cheerful and unconcerned about visiting her quite openly at the No. 1 Ladies' Detective Agency. It was strange.

"It is good to see you, Rra," she said. "And I'm happy to see you here in the office. Last time, you seemed unwilling . . ."

Mr. Moeti looked at her suspiciously. "What last time? What unwilling?"

Mma Ramotswe watched him carefully. Her remark had wrong-footed him, she thought. That was interesting; had he forgotten? Actors forget; people who are not acting never do.

"Last time you consulted me," she said. "You didn't want to come to the office. And forgive me if I say this, Rra, but you seemed very anxious then. Are you no longer worried?"

For a moment or two he said nothing. He's thinking, she said to herself; thinking what to say.

He looked over his shoulder—an exaggerated glance. "I am still worried, Mma. And wouldn't you be, if you knew that somebody was trying to harm you? Even during the day, things can happen . . ."

He transferred his gaze to the window, looking out as if to identify any threat lurking outside. From where she was sitting, if she half turned in her seat, Mma Ramotswe could not see a great deal, but she had a good view of the sky, which was empty, innocent. A shadow passed over his face, though; she could see its effect in his eyes.

"You have reminded me, Mma Ramotswe," he said quietly. "I had almost forgotten, and I was happy. But you have reminded me."

She had not expected this, and his comment made her catch her breath. Perhaps he really was frightened, and perhaps she had tactlessly spoiled things for him. *He is my client,* she reminded herself. *He is not a suspect.*

"I'm very sorry, Rra," she said. "It is not my business to tell you how you're feeling."

The apology was accepted with a quick movement of the hands. "That's all right, Mma. No damage. It's best to be positive, I find, and that's what I'm trying to do. We cannot let wicked people spoil our lives for us, can we?"

Mma Ramotswe indicated that she agreed with this sentiment. And she did; stopping wicked people from spoiling the lives of the non-wicked was, after all, what she and Mma Makutsi did in their working lives.

"So," went on Mr. Moeti, "tell me, Mma: What have you found out? Have you any . . . what do you people call them? Any *leads*?"

Mr. Moeti's use of the word *lead* was a godsend to Mma Ramotswe. She had an answer, not a lead, so she replied, "No leads as such, Rra."

He did not seem unduly disappointed. "Well, I have."

She looked at him politely. "Oh yes, Rra? What have you found out?"

He sat back in his chair. "You remember that thing we found? The key ring?"

She nodded: the cheap metal map of Botswana.

"I have found out where it is from."

"Who dropped it?"

He hesitated. "No, not directly, but I have found out which firm gives them to its business clients. There is a firm of livestock-feed manufacturers in Lobatse. They make that lick that you give to cattle."

Mma Ramotswe knew the lick in question. She used it herself out at her cattle post. Cattle loved the salt it contained, and it gave them all sorts of other things too. Of course humans were rather like cattle these days, she thought—always taking extra vitamin pills. Perhaps they should make a vitamin lick for people, which they could put on people's floors, and they would get down on all fours and lick away, just like cattle.

"So, Rra," she said. "You have found out who gives the key ring away. But you have not found out who owned this particular key ring, have you? Is that correct?"

Mr. Moeti reached forward and tapped the desk lightly. "No, I have not done that because that would be impossible, Mma Ramotswe. Nobody, not even the best detective in the world, could look at a key ring and say that it belonged to this person or that person. But . . ."

He was looking at her with a curious intensity; she held his gaze. "Yes?"

"But I can tell you something about this key ring, Mma—something that will make you sit up straight in your chair."

Mma Ramotswe shifted slightly. Had she been slouching? Perhaps it was just the impression that her chair gave—it had always sagged in the middle, for some reason.

"Yes," continued Mr. Moeti. "I know that the firm that gives away this key ring is in Lobatse. I know that it makes cattle-lick. And I know who owns it."

Mma Ramotswe nodded politely. "That is a lot to know, Rra. But what has it got to do with our inquiry?"

"It is the person who owns that firm that will interest you. He is my neighbour."

Mma Ramotswe digested this information. "So are you saying that he must have dropped it?"

There was a look of undisguised triumph on Mr. Moeti's face. "Exactly. That is exactly what I am saying. This thing—this attack on my cattle—was carried out by my neighbour."

He paused, watching the effect of his disclosure. From the other side of the office there came a muttered comment: "Neighbour! It is always the neighbour!"

Mr. Moeti turned in his seat and stared at Mma Makutsi.

"My assistant," said Mma Ramotswe. "As she told you, she is an—"

"Associate detective," supplied Mma Makutsi.

Mr. Moeti nodded. "Very good," he said. "And you are right, Mma Makutsi. It is always the neighbour who is the problem."

"Except sometimes," Mma Ramotswe said gently, "some neighbours are no trouble at all. Many, in fact."

"That may be true," said Mr. Moeti. "But not in this case. This neighbour of mine is big trouble. Big trouble. It should have been obvious to me that he was suspect number one. I don't know why I didn't think of it."

The way he said that he did not know why he had not thought of it struck Mma Ramotswe as very strange. It was said flatly, as a bad actor will deliver a line in an unaccented monotone.

"But we need a motive, Rra," she said.

This, by contrast, brought an energetic reply. "Motive? He is a bad man, Mma. Bad men always have motives—plenty of motives, I think."

She wanted to find out in what respects this neighbour—still nameless—was bad. "You must tell me about him, Rra," she said. "His name first, and then why you have this low opinion of him."

"He is called Fortitude Seleo," Mr. Moeti began.

He uttered the name with an expression of disgust, or as one might talk if one were obliged to speak with a slice of bitter lemon in one's mouth. Or carbolic soap. Carbolic soap had been administered to children who used bad language when Mma Ramotswe had been young. The miscreant's mouth had been opened and a sliver of soap applied to the tongue and palate while others looked on. And the punished child would pull a face and run off to the taps to rinse out the offending mouth. It had been effective, she remembered, and although one could never do such a thing today, she could not help but notice that people used bad language casually and with no regard to the feelings of others. There would not be carbolic soap enough, she thought, to clean up the language used in films, where people found it necessary to curse and swear with utter abandon. Mma Potokwane would have views on this, she imagined; none of the children at the orphan farm used such language. Love, not punishment—that was the solution; the sort of love that Mma Potokwane could dispense to scores of children: a brisk, understanding love; a love that made them want to do their best and make the most of a world that had treated them badly at the start of their young lives.

"Fortitude Seleo," she said.

"Yes, that is the man, Mma. He owns that factory and he thinks that because he is a big manufacturer of cattle-lick he can have the whole country for his own cattle." He paused. "And so when his fences fall down he doesn't bother to fix them, but lets them wander wherever they like. They could go into the middle of Gaborone and start grazing on the lawn of the Grand Palms Hotel for all he cared!

"But do his cattle catch a bus and ride into Gaborone for their breakfast? No, they do not, Mma. They just wander onto his neighbour's land—that is me, by the way—and eat and eat there until all the grass is eaten up. Then they go back and are sent down to Lobatse for slaughter with their stomachs full of my grass! That is what happens, Mma. It has happened four times, five times, one hundred times maybe.

"And what does he do when I phone him and tell him that his cattle are on my land? He says, 'Are you sure, Rra? Because I do not think any of my cattle are missing. Maybe you should get your herd boy to check. Maybe he is just making these things up.' That is what he has the cheek to say to me, Mma Ramotswe. He thinks I am just some ignorant man who doesn't know what's going on. He thinks that he can fob me off with this nonsense."

The diatribe continued. "I took him to the broken fence one day and pointed out where it was lying on the ground like some old fence from the Protectorate days. Some old British fence maybe. And I said to him, 'Look here, what is this? Is this not your fence?' And he said, 'That fence is your fence, Rra. That fence is your responsibility and you should be fixing it rather than me. Do not tell me to fix a fence that is not mine or anything to do with me.' Those were his actual words, Mma. That is what he said. And I had to take a big breath because I was so angry that I had forgotten to breathe and all my oxygen was gone. He is a man who makes you use up all your oxygen when you are with him, Mma. It is not just me, I assure you. There are many people who have run out of oxygen when arguing with that man. Maybe that is the way he wants it—maybe that is his technique. He makes people run out of oxygen, and then they fall over and he has won. There are people like that, Mma—I'm sure you know that as well as I do."

Mma Ramotswe sat quite still. There was an eloquence to this denunciation that was as alarming as it was impressive. And even if Mr. Moeti had almost run out of oxygen when arguing with Fortitude Seleo, there seemed to be no danger of that happening now.

"He would not accept," Mr. Moeti went on, "that the fences were his. I said that I would look at the title to the land and check up on what it said about fences, and he said that titles were drawn up by lawyers and what did lawyers know about fences? How can you argue with a man like that, Mma? I couldn't, and so I just had to chase his cattle off my land and wait until it happened again. And again after that.

"He is a greedy man, that man. Very large, Mma. Not that there is anything wrong in being large, I must say. It is a good thing to be large; it shows that the country is prosperous. I am just saying that sometimes people can be a little bit too large because they have eaten a bit too much beef. That is the case with Seleo, I think. The country is not big enough for him, he thinks, Mma. There really need to be two Botswanas—one for Mr. Fortitude Seleo and one for the rest of us Batswana. Two whole countries. And then his cattle would start wandering out of his private Botswana and coming over to eat the grass in our Botswana. That would happen, Mma, I have absolutely no doubt about it. It is definite. His cattle have got a very bad temperament, Mma. They are like their owner. They are arrogant. Arrogant man, arrogant cattle. That is definite, Mma. Definite."

He sat back in his chair and folded his arms with the air of one who has proved his case. Mma Ramotswe waited for a few moments to see if he had anything further to say, but he had not.

"So, Rra," she began. "You do not like this Mr. Seleo."

Mr. Moeti shook his head, but remained mute.

"Well," continued Mma Ramotswe, "it sounds to me as if he is not the best of neighbours, but that does not mean that he—"

"Of course he did it," interrupted Mr. Moeti. "We found his key ring at the scene. That is big proof."

Mma Ramotswe was tactful, but felt that she had to spell out just what was meant by real proof. "You have to ask yourself what a clue means," she said. "What does it say to you? That is the question you must ask."

"It says to me: this man Seleo attacked my cattle. That's what it says to me."

Mma Makutsi, who had been following this exchange with rapt attention, now intervened. "It says: somebody has dropped a key ring. That is all it says. It does not say whose key ring has been dropped. It could be anybody's."

Mr. Moeti did not turn to face Mma Makutsi, but addressed her while still looking at Mma Ramotswe. "Seleo makes that key ring. It is his key ring. He does not like me, or my cattle. He drops his key ring after he has done his wicked deed. Anybody can tell that."

It was clear that Mma Makutsi was irritated by being addressed by one facing the other way. "I hope you can hear me, Rra," she said. "I think sometimes that when you talk to the back of somebody's head they do not hear you because their ears are facing the other way."

Mma Ramotswe raised a cautionary finger, but Mma Makutsi continued undaunted. "That is why it is not only polite, but also wise to face the person who is talking to you—that way you don't miss anything. That is just one view, of course, but it is significant, I think, that it is the view held by all polite people in Botswana." She paused. There was more to come. "Of course, there may be countries where things are done quite differently. I do not know, for instance, whether it is customary to talk to the back of people's heads in China. For all I know that might be considered quite polite and normal; but I do know that this is not the case in Botswana."

Mma Ramotswe looked down at the desk. It was hard to stop Mma Makutsi once she had started, and it was particularly difficult to do so now that she was about to become Mrs. Phuti Radiphuti and would shortly have no financial need of the job, even if she had indicated that she wanted to continue working.

Mr. Moeti had now turned, slowly and awkwardly, so that he was facing Mma Makutsi. He looked embarrassed.

"So the point is this, Rra," Mma Makutsi went on. "There will be many key rings of that sort. The fact is that we cannot link *that* key ring to Mr. Seleo. So we have nothing against him, other than that he and you are not friends."

Mr. Moeti turned round again to face Mma Ramotswe. "So you and that lady behind me, Mma, have nothing to report."

"We will be looking very carefully into the whole thing," said Mma Ramotswe. "We shall consider every aspect of the situation." She spread her hands. "At present, we do not really have anything concrete, but I shall certainly look into your suggestion that it is this Seleo man who has done this dreadful thing."

This seemed to satisfy Mr. Moeti, who nodded enthusiastically. "Good," he said. "And then, when we catch him, Mma, we can tell the world what sort of man he is and how I have been putting up with his nonsense for such a long time. That will be very good."

Mr. Moeti departed, taking great care to say an elaborate farewell to Mma Makutsi as he left. Once they were alone, Mma Ramotswe and Mma Makutsi exchanged glances across the room.

"A very rude man," said Mma Makutsi. "But what can we expect these days? The world has forgotten about manners."

"Yes, sometimes it seems like that, Mma, and then you suddenly come across somebody with good manners and you realise that there are still people who believe in these things." She paused. "Like your Phuti. He has very good manners—old Botswana manners."

Mma Makutsi beamed at her employer. "Oh, Mma, thank you. I think you are quite right."

"Yes, I am," said Mma Ramotswe. "I think Phuti would have got on very well with my Daddy. I am sure of it, in fact. They would have been very good friends, I believe."

Mma Makutsi knew that this was the highest possible praise from Mma Ramotswe. "It is a shame that they cannot meet," she said. "Since your father is late, that will no longer be possible, but it would have been a very good thing had it been able to happen."

They sat in silence for a moment, both imagining the scene of that meeting: Obed Ramotswe, with his battered old hat and his face that had such understanding and kindness etched into every line of it; Phuti Radiphuti, with his slightly ill-fitting suit and his artificial foot, but with his polite and gentle manner. It would, thought Mma Ramotswe, have been an embodiment, an affirmation, of everything that Botswana stood for: decency and the things that decency brought with it.

Mma Ramotswe brought the spell to an end. "There's something odd going on, Mma Makutsi," she said.

"Very odd, Mma Ramotswe. And in my opinion it is that man who is odd. He is lying, if you ask me."

Mma Ramotswe said that she, too, had the impression that Mr.

Moeti was not being truthful, but what exactly was he lying about? Was he lying about his neighbour? Was he inventing the story of the fence, which would, of course, be a gross defamation of his neighbour's cattle? "I just can't work it out, Mma Makutsi," she said. "But one thing I think is very clear: that man was never frightened. He had been pretending to be frightened, but his fear was not real."

"You are right," said Mma Makutsi. "He was not a frightened man. A rude man, yes, but not a frightened one."

"And that Fortitude Seleo?"

Mma Makutsi thought for a moment. "I would like to think he is an ordinary man who has the misfortune to have a farm next to Moeti's farm. That is what I'd like to think, Mma. But what I actually think is quite different."

Mma Ramotswe looked expectantly at her assistant. "Yes, Mma. What do you think?"

"I think that he's probably very rude too," said Mma Makutsi. "So put two cats in a box and what do they do, Mma? They fight."

CHAPTER THIRTEEN

WAS PRUDENCE PRUDENT?

PRUDENCE RAMKHWANE lived with her parents, Leonard and Mercy, in a large house behind the shopping centre at the beginning of the Lobatse road. It was not a good place to live, thought Mma Ramotswe, who did not like the clutter and noise of that particular conglomeration of shops, but there were those who did, she had to remind herself, and there must also be those who did not mind living close to such places.

As she parked her car outside the Ramkhwane gate, Mma Ramotswe found herself looking at the house with her detective's eye. This was a special way of looking at things that she had developed over the years, not without some assistance from the relevant chapter of Clovis Andersen's *The Principles of Private Detection*. The author of that seminal work had sound advice in this regard. *Always remember that things are where they are because somebody has put them there,* he wrote. *So if there is a kennel in a yard it is there because the owner of the yard put it there, and that means that he has a dog. If there is a boat in the yard, then you may conclude that he likes fishing. Things are always there for a reason. I learned this les-*

son myself from Mrs. Andersen, who always accuses me of moving things that she needs!

It was a lovely, intimate glimpse into the home life of the great authority, and Mma Ramotswe had read the passage aloud to Mma Makutsi, who had enjoyed it a great deal.

"How interesting to hear about his wife," Mma Makutsi said. "I would not have guessed that he was married, but there you are."

"She must be very proud of him," said Mma Ramotswe. "It must be strange to be married to such a famous man."

"I expect she's used to it," said Mma Makutsi. "And she probably talks to him like any wife, telling him to be careful and to watch what he does and so on."

Mma Ramotswe had smiled at this. "Is that how you think wives talk, Mma?" she asked. "If so, you should be careful when you and Phuti get married. Men don't like being told to watch what they do."

"But if we let them do what they wanted, then what would happen?" asked Mma Makutsi. "It would be chaos. Big chaos."

Mma Ramotswe had agreed that it would not be a good idea to allow men to do as they pleased, but she felt that there were tactful ways of achieving the desired result. "Rather than telling a man directly what to do," she said, "a wife should make the man think that he is doing what *he* wants to do. There are ways of making this happen, Mma—tactful ways."

There had then followed a certain amount of instruction on how to handle husbands, during which Mma Makutsi made the occasional note.

"This will be very useful for when I am married," she told Mma Ramotswe, and then added, "And I think you should possibly write a book, Mma. It could be called *How to Handle Husbands and Keep Them Under Control.* Or something like that. It would be a very successful book, Mma, as there are many ladies who would rush to buy a book like that."

Now, standing in front of the Ramkhwane house, Mma Ramotswe looked about the yard to determine what it said about the Ramkhwane family. The yard was well swept, which was a good sign—indeed, the most important message that a householder could send out was that based on the neatness, or otherwise, of the yard. Then there was the car: that spoke to modesty—a modest person drives a modest car, a pushy person drives a pushy car. The Ramkhwane car was unostentatious, she was pleased to note: a medium-sized vehicle painted white—a traditional Botswana colour for a car and completely unobjectionable for that. And at the back of the yard, a vegetable patch and a hen coop—both good signs of traditional Botswana values.

Good manners would have required that she call out from the gate and await an invitation before entering the yard. That was difficult to do, though, when the gate was some distance from the house as this one was, so she made her way towards the front door, a large, red-painted affair with an elaborate brass knocker fixed to its central panel.

A maid answered—a thin, rather lethargic woman in a faded print smock. Unhappy, thought Mma Ramotswe. There would be a hundred possible reasons for her unhappiness, but it was probably something to do with poverty and the bad behaviour of some man somewhere—just as was the case with the maid at Mr. Moeti's place.

"I have come to see Prudence, Mma," said Mma Ramotswe. "I think this is her house."

The woman gave a reply that sounded like a sigh. "Yes, Mma. This is her place."

The maid gestured to Mma Ramotswe that she should follow

her. They went along a corridor and into a room at the side of the house. It was a sparsely furnished bedroom with a large cot. Two babies under a year old were sleeping in the cot, one at each end, their small rounded stomachs exposed. In a chair by the window, reading a magazine, was a young woman in jeans and T-shirt. This was Prudence.

Prudence looked up in surprise.

"I have come to see you," said Mma Ramotswe. "My name is Precious Ramotswe. I know . . ." She glanced at the babies. Should she say, *I know their father?* She decided to say, "I know Charlie."

Prudence looked away. She had not got up when Mma Ramotswe had entered, in spite of the difference in their ages. "Oh yes," she said flatly. "Charlie. How is he?"

"He is very well," said Mma Ramotswe.

There was a silence. Then Mma Ramotswe spoke again: "I think you must be cross with him."

Prudence looked up sharply. "Cross with Charlie? Why should I be cross with Charlie?"

Mma Ramotswe glanced at the twins. "The babies . . ."

Prudence stared at her. "What have they got to do with it?"

Mma Ramotswe was perplexed. "I thought . . . I heard that Charlie was the father. That is what I heard."

Prudence frowned. "Charlie? Oh no, Charlie is not the father. No, it is not him."

"Some other man then?"

Prudence flicked a page of her magazine. "Yes, some other man. He is a pilot. He flies up in Maun—those small planes that go to the safari camps. He is Kenyan. We're going to get married in a few months—at long last."

"Does Charlie know this?" asked Mma Ramotswe.

"About me getting married?"

"Yes. About the twins . . . and this other man, this Kenyan."

Prudence shrugged. "He doesn't think he's the father of the babies, does he?"

Mma Ramotswe explained that Charlie had drawn that conclusion, and that was why there had been a rather sudden termination of the relationship.

Prudence listened to her with interest, but without any great show of emotion. "Well, he's wrong," she said once Mma Ramotswe had finished. "I never told him he was the father. I told him I was pregnant—that's all." She looked at Mma Ramotswe to see if she had grasped the distinction. "Listen, Mma, the point is that I had more than one boyfriend then. I know you shouldn't, but it's difficult sometimes when there are all these men knocking on the door. What are you expected to do?"

Mma Ramotswe was about to say, *You choose one and you stick to him,* but she judged it best not to engage. There would be no point in getting into an argument about faithfulness with Prudence; it was too late for her to change, she thought. And there were other people who should tackle her about that.

But she could not let the matter pass altogether. "But you told your parents that Charlie was the father?"

Prudence looked away sulkily. "I didn't say that, Mma. Not exactly. Maybe they thought it themselves—because I was seeing Charlie at the time."

"And they didn't know about the other man . . . or men?"

Prudence shrugged. "Maybe not."

Mma Ramotswe stared at her. She found it hard to imagine such callousness. She sighed. "I don't think you behaved very well, Mma," she said gently.

Prudence looked at her blankly. Perhaps she simply does not understand, thought Mma Ramotswe. Something was missing.

"Oh well, Mma," she said, "I think that I should be on my way. Charlie says hello, by the way."

"Tell him hello," said Prudence. "Tell him that I think of him a lot. Tell him to come and see me some time, but to phone first."

"I shall," said Mma Ramotswe.

"And if you'd like something to eat," Prudence went on, "I can get you something."

Mma Ramotswe raised an eyebrow. "Thank you, Mma, but I am not hungry." She paused. One of the babies had stirred, but only to move an arm. "They are very fine babies, Mma. You must be proud of them."

"They eat a lot," said Prudence. "And I'm having another one, you know."

Mma Ramotswe looked at her watch. "I really must go, Mma. I have a lot of work to do." She did not, but she wanted to leave the house; she wanted to be away from this silly young woman with her casual ways and her utter indifference. How could anybody be so *bored* with life, she wondered, when all about one there were all these *things* happening?

The maid showed her out. As they approached the front door, Mma Ramotswe leaned over and whispered, "Mma, that girl, Prudence, doesn't seem to care very much about things, does she?"

There was a flicker across the maid's otherwise impassive face. "She is seeing two men. Two men, Mma! One is the man who is going to marry her, the other is another man altogether. I know these things; I see them."

Mma Ramotswe shook her head. "It is very bad."

"She is a bad girl," said the maid. "It is very unfair, Mma. She has all this—she has her good parents and she has their money, their food. And all the time she is bad. It is unfair, Mma."

Mma Ramotswe reached out and took the maid's hand. "Do

not feel too sad about it, my sister," she said. "I know what you mean."

The maid looked down at the floor. "Sometimes I think that God has forgotten about me," she said.

Mma Ramotswe shook her head. "He hasn't, Mma," she whispered. "You must never think that. His love is always there, Mma, always there. And it doesn't matter who we are—if we are poor people or people who have been badly treated—we are every bit as important in God's eyes as anybody else. Every bit."

The maid listened, but said nothing.

"You heard me, did you, Mma?" asked Mma Ramotswe.

The other woman nodded. "I heard you, Mma."

Mma Ramotswe reached into the pocket of her skirt. Fifty pula—not a small sum. "This is a present, Mma," she said, pressing the banknote into the woman's hand. "No, you must take it. I want you to have it."

The maid tucked the note away. "I have a little boy," she said.

"Then tonight he will have a very good meal, I think," said Mma Ramotswe.

For the first time, the maid smiled.

SHE RETURNED DIRECTLY to the No. 1 Ladies' Detective Agency. Parking her van under the tree, she went not into the office but into the garage, where Mr. J.L.B. Matekoni's legs, together with two other sets of legs, all clad in blue overalls, protruded from under a large green truck. She called out to her husband, who answered from below the vehicle.

"This is a very tricky repair, Mma," he shouted out, his voice sounding distant under the truck. "I am doing my best, but it is very, very tricky."

"I do not want to disturb you, Rra," she shouted back. "I need to talk to Charlie."

"I am watching Mr. J.L.B. Matekoni, Mma," Charlie called out.

"You can go, Charlie," said Mr. J.L.B. Matekoni. "Fanwell and I can manage all right."

She watched as Charlie wiggled out from under the truck. He had, she noticed, a large fresh oil stain on the bib of his overalls. She tut-tutted. "You will have to put those in the wash, Charlie. Oil is a very difficult thing. Soak them first, then put them in the wash."

He looked down unconcernedly at the stain. "Oil is nothing, Mma. I do not mind." He looked at her inquisitively. "What do you want, Mma?"

She drew him aside. "I offered to help you, Charlie. Remember?"

He became nervous. His hands shook slightly; you would have to be looking for it, but she noticed it.

"Yes, Mma, you did."

"And I have done that," she went on. "I have been to see Prudence."

She saw his lip was now quivering.

"Yes, Mma?"

"Let me tell you this straightaway, Charlie. You are not the father of those twins. It is another man."

He stared at her wide-eyed. "I am not . . ."

"No," said Mma Ramotswe. "You see, that girl, Prudence, is very friendly with men. She should watch out."

Charlie started to smile. "I am not the father? Is this true?"

"She thinks it is," said Mma Ramotswe. "And what the mother thinks tends to be the most important thing, I think."

The news seemed to be sinking in slowly. "I do not have twins?"

"You do not."

Charlie shook his head in disbelief. "I am going to be different from now on, Mma Ramotswe. You'll see. I'm going to be different."

"In what way, Charlie?"

"In every way, Mma. I am going to be a different man. More careful. Just one girlfriend. That's all. A better mechanic too."

She looked at him. For all his faults—and she had to admit they were manifold—he was a well-meaning young man. And much as he could be frustrating, he could also be amusing and generous and attractive.

"Don't change too much," she said gently. "We like you the way you are, Charlie."

He stared at her incredulously, and she realised that he might not have heard many people say that. So she repeated herself: "We like you, Charlie; you just remember that."

She looked down. He had clasped his hands together, his fingers interlaced. It was a gesture, she thought, of unequivocal pleasure—pleasure at hearing what all of us wanted to hear at least occasionally: that there was somebody who liked us, whatever our faults, and liked us sufficiently to say so.

CHAPTER FOURTEEN

A GOOD MAN, A KIND MAN

WHAT, Mma Ramotswe asked herself, did she know about Mr. Fortitude Seleo?

The answer to this question was brief. She knew that he had a factory that made cattle-lick; she knew that this factory was in Lobatse; and she knew that he was the neighbour of her client, Mr. Botsalo Moeti. That was all that she actually *knew.* The rest was all gossip and allegations from a single source—Mr. Moeti himself, who did not like Mr. Seleo, and, more significantly, did not like his cattle. That thought itself led to further surmise: if Moeti did not like Seleo's cattle, then it was odd, was it not, that Moeti's cattle had been attacked, rather than the other way round. There would have been a clear motive had that happened: Seleo's cattle had a habit of trespassing on Moeti's land; if Seleo's cattle were attacked, then the finger of suspicion would surely point at Moeti.

But what if the truth were rather different from the story as told by Moeti? What if Moeti's cattle had been every bit as lawless as Seleo's cattle and had themselves crossed over onto Seleo's land? Then Seleo would have had a clear motive to wreak his revenge on the poor beasts. That made sense of what had happened. Seleo had been angry over the incursions and had taken action. Moeti knew why his neighbour had done this, but had kept this knowledge from Mma Ramotswe—presumably to appear more of the innocent victim.

Then a disturbing possibility suggested itself: she had been treating Mr. Moeti as the victim, but it was possible that he was, in fact, the perpetrator. That would mean, of course, that he had attacked his own cattle, something that no farmer would dream of doing—unless he did not know that they *were* his cattle.

She pictured it. Night-time, and the herd boy, young Mpho, knocks urgently on the door of the farmhouse. "Who is it?" calls Moeti. "His cattle have broken through the fence, Rra. You must come." Moeti comes to the door, belting his trousers, cursing under his breath. He runs to his truck; Mpho, shivering, sits in the back. They drive along the bumpy track; the stars are bright overhead, the moon nowhere to be seen; the headlamps cut into the darkness, and then there is just the dark hump of the hills in the distance. The cattle eyes are yellow points caught in the lights; they lift their heads and move off into the darkness. Two stragglers. Moeti shouts and there is bellowing. The blood cannot be seen because of the dark. He shouts at the boy again and returns to the truck and they are gone and do not hear the crying of the injured beasts.

And in the morning he discovers that his own cattle were mixed up with the neighbour's herd, and he has maimed his own beast, and he vents his fury on the boy, and beats him. "You are not to say anything about this, understand? Nothing!" The idea occurs to him that he should blame somebody else—his neighbour, whose fault this really was. Let old scores be settled; put somebody on to him—not the police, because he would talk his way out of that and was friendly with the local policeman, but get somebody from outside, somebody accepting Moeti's money and answerable to him alone.

Of course, all of this implied that Mpho's confession was false, and of that she was simply unsure. One moment she thought that the boy was probably telling the truth, the next she found herself inclined to think that he had made it up too quickly, or was lying to protect somebody else. And would a small boy, she wondered, have thought up something so devilish as to attack cattle in this way? Surely not.

She was driving to see Fortitude Seleo when she thought this, and the train of thought was so compelling that she almost stopped her van in order to sit still and think the matter through. But then, as is often the case with good ideas, the obvious flaw appeared, and so she continued with her drive. The flaw arose from what Mr. Moeti had said to her of the events. There had been two attacks, he said—the second one just a week before their first meeting. This ruled out the possibility that he had mistakenly attacked one of his own animals: he would never have made the same mistake twice. That was unlikely, she had to admit—unless, of course, the second attack had never occurred and had simply been invented to make the situation seem more serious.

She made an effort to stop thinking about it. Sometimes, she found, it was better to defer deliberations of that sort until the end of a case, when you had to hand all the information you were going to get and could put the jigsaw together without suddenly finding fresh pieces. And she had almost reached her destination—the premises of the not very imaginatively named Botswana Cattle Food Company, from the chimneys of which emanated wisps of steam, rising up in short-lived spouts and clouds. A large truck, painted with the name of the company, was reversing towards a loading bay and a security guard, bespectacled and officious, was approaching the van.

The guard told her where to park before directing her to the front office. He noted her name on his clipboard and smiled at her. "You have many cattle, Mma?" he asked.

She nodded. "I have a cattle post. My father—he is late now—was good with them. He was a fine judge of cattle."

"I have cattle too," he said. "Not many. Three. Out there." He waved a hand in the direction of the Kalahari.

She hesitated. She did not like to miss opportunities to talk to people, as this was the way one found things out. This guard must know Mr. Seleo; if she wanted to find out about his employer, then she should chat to him. Security guards, cleaners, porters—these were the ones who often knew what people were really like.

"I have come to see Rra Seleo," she said.

The guard beamed. "Yes. If you go to the office, you will find him. He is always there."

"You must know him well," she said. "I have never met him."

"Yes. You will meet him, Mma. He will be there."

She tried again. "What's he like?"

"You will see, Mma. If you ask at the office, they will take you to him. He is over there."

It was not working. "Thank you, Rra. I'll go there."

He began to walk with her. "So you haven't met him, Mma?"

"No."

"He is a good man. A kind man."

"Kind? Why do you say he's kind, Rra? Usually these businessmen are tough, aren't they? You do not find many kind people running businesses these days, I think."

The guard considered this gravely before replying. "I don't know about that, Mma. Perhaps you are right; I am just an ordinary man and do not know about these things. But I can tell you about Mr. Seleo. He never shouts. He never fires people if they are late for work. You don't see him chasing after the young secretaries—there is none of that here."

Mma Ramotswe smiled. "I am glad to hear that, Rra. There is too much of those things going on in Gaborone. I'm glad that it is not happening here."

"Yes, Mma. I'm glad too."

They had reached the door to the office, and the guard opened it for her before he went back to his post at the gate. Mma Ramotswe thanked him and made her way over to a reception desk. A young woman took her name and lifted the telephone. She spoke briefly, and then pointed to a door on the other side of the room.

"That is where he is," she said. "In there."

MR. FORTITUDE SELEO was a tall, well-built man somewhere in his mid-fifties, or a bit beyond. His hair was greying and his face was lined about the eyes and mouth. When he stood up to greet Mma Ramotswe, she immediately saw the reason for the lines: a broad smile spread across his face.

"Mma Ramotswe," he said. "I am very happy to meet you, Mma. You are well, I hope."

It was an effusive greeting, and it took Mma Ramotswe slightly aback. But she recovered quickly and returned the smile.

"I am very well, Rra. Thank you. And you are well?"

"Very well too, Mma Ramotswe. Very well. And glad that winter is over."

"I am glad too, Rra."

He indicated the chair in front of his desk, and she sat down.

"So, Mma, you are the great detective, aren't you? I have heard about you—even down here."

Mma Ramotswe's embarrassment was unfeigned. "I didn't think that people knew about me, Rra. I am not famous."

"No, perhaps not famous, Mma. But people driving along the Tlokweng Road see your sign. What is it, Mma? The No Ladies Detective Agency? That makes them think: Who are these no ladies?"

"It is the No. 1 Ladies' Detective Agency, Rra."

Mr. Seleo laughed. "Oh, I see. But that is how people know about you." He paused, watching her, his smile still broad. "So why have you come to see me, Mma? Is it something to do with my friend Botsalo Moeti? Something to do with a dead cow?"

Clovis Andersen was quite clear on this: do not let your reactions show. Control your feelings. Do not look excessively surprised or dismayed.

Mma Ramotswe felt both of these emotions. "Oh," she said lamely. "So, you know."

He seemed concerned about the effect of his words. "I'm sorry, Mma," he said quickly, his smile fading. "I did not mean to take you by surprise."

"I did not think that you knew," Mma Ramotswe said.

"Knew what?"

"That you knew that I was interested in this affair."

Mr. Seleo leaned back in his chair. The smile and jovial manner had both returned. "Oh, I knew all right," he said. "In the country we all know what's going on, Mma. I heard about your visit. The bush has eyes, you know."

"And those eyes were watching me," said Mma Ramotswe.

"They were."

He looked at her with complete affability and equability; the security guard, she thought, must be absolutely right.

"I'm afraid," continued Mr. Seleo, "that relations between me and my neighbour are not all that I would wish them to be. It is so important, Mma, to get on with your neighbours—as I'm sure you are very well aware."

"It is very important indeed," agreed Mma Ramotswe. "A fight with a neighbour is like a fight in your own home. Almost as bad."

He considered this. "Yes, I think I'd agree. And for this reason I did my best to get on with Botsalo Moeti. I really did. But his cattle kept coming onto my land, and I had to take the matter up with him. I did so as gently as possible—I invited him round for a meal, and my wife made a great big stew and lots of trimmings. I raised the issue as tactfully as I could, but he flew off the handle, Mma. He went off like a firework."

It was exactly as she had imagined in the car; or at least this part of it was. And there was no question in her mind now as to whom she believed and as to whose cattle had wandered.

"There has been a whole lot of things since then," Mr. Seleo explained. "It seems that he's a man who just has to settle scores. If he thinks that you've done something to him, then he will attempt to get back at you. It's quite extraordinary, Mma Ramotswe. So along comes this business with the cow—somebody does something nasty to one of his cows and he gets the idea that this is his chance to even things up with me. I'm not at all surprised that he's trying to pin the attack on me—that's the way he is, I'm afraid."

She sat in silence once he had finished. Mma Ramotswe was usually positive in her outlook, but now she felt somewhat bleak. There were some people who would never change—they seemed irredeemably malevolent. Fortunately there were few of these, but you did come across them from time to time, and then you felt strangely dirtied by the contact.

After a while she spoke. "I am very sorry, Rra," she said. "I am very sorry that I even thought that you might be responsible for such a thing."

Mr. Seleo shrugged. "You were only doing your job, Mma. I don't hold anything against you."

"So what do we do about Mr. Moeti?"

The smile did not slip. "We have to live with him, Mma. What else can we do?"

She could not think of anything else to say, so she brought the conversation round to cattle-lick. She had used his lick and her cattle loved it. They could not say thank you, of course, but she could on their behalf. This made Mr. Seleo burst into peals of laughter.

"Oh, Mma," he said, "that is extremely amusing. You are the spokesman for the cattle of Botswana! And have the cattle got anything further to say? Are they happy with conditions in general?"

She thought for a moment. Were the cattle of Botswana happy? "I think they are," she said. And then she became more definite. "Yes, they certainly are." She hesitated. "Or most of them."

An idea had occurred to her. It was not the most obvious idea, and she was not sure whether it would work. Happiness, she thought, is a healer, and could sometimes shift a log-jam in the most seemingly impossible circumstances. In every human heart, even the most forbidding, there was a place that could be touched. The difficulty was finding it; there were people who concealed that place with dogged determination. Sometimes, though, their guard slipped for a moment or two, and the way to a heart lay open.

Mr. Seleo showed her out, saying that he would walk her to her van.

"Tell me, Rra," she said. "Would you do something to end this dispute with your neighbour?"

"Of course," he said. "But what can I do? The fences that he complains of are his, not mine. His cattle keep coming over onto my land. It's not my fault."

"But what if that were to stop?"

"Then I wouldn't have to talk to him about it. It would not be a problem."

"And do you have to talk to him about it often?"

He thought for a moment. "Every few days I have to telephone him. Or I go over to see him at his place." He paused. "But I am always polite, Mma."

She told him that she was sure he was. But then she thought: How easy would it be to get annoyed by a neighbour—even a smiling, agreeable one like this—who kept raising an issue with you, day after day? Very easy, she thought.

"Perhaps you should think of stopping that, Rra. Just for a while. Perhaps that would help."

There was a sudden and very obvious change in Mr. Seleo's demeanour. The smile was still there, of course, but the light had gone from it; it was frozen. "Why should I, Mma? I am in the right here, you know."

"I don't doubt that, Rra, but I think . . ."

He waited for her to finish. What did she think, and how should she put it? They were standing outside the main building of the factory, now, and she turned to face the building, looking up at the hissing steam pipes. There was a pleasant smell in the air—rather like the smell of baking cakes.

"I think we could sort this out," she said. "But it will require you to swallow your pride."

He looked at her intently. "I am not a proud man, Mma."

"Good," she said. "So, Rra, would you like me to tell you what I think you should do? You may not like it, but I think it may be the solution to this problem you have. But I need first to ask you something. Does Mr. Moeti look after his cattle well?"

He raised an eyebrow. "That's a difficult question for me, Mma."

"Why? Do you not know?"

"No, I know perfectly well. It's just that I do not like to speak ill of people, Mma, especially when it comes to the way they treat their cattle."

There was no doubt in her mind that he meant it. This man, she thought, really is a good man. "You are very right about that, Rra," she said. "We should not speak badly about people—except where we have to. And this is one of those occasions. I have to know."

"Terribly," he blurted out. "He's hopeless—a hopeless farmer. He has no idea how to look after cattle. He thinks he does, but he doesn't, I'm afraid. Just look at the condition of his herd."

It was the answer for which she had hoped. "So that's why they wander?"

He nodded. "Yes, and if I were one of his cows I would move on. I'd emigrate to Namibia, maybe."

Mma Ramotswe laughed, and then asked a further question. "Your cattle, of course, are happy, I imagine."

"Yes. They are in very good condition."

"They get plenty of healthy cattle-lick? Cattle-lick with all the right things? Vitamins, magnesium, salt—all those other things that cattle need?"

This broadened his smile. "Yes, as you can imagine."

"And his cattle get none?"

He shrugged. "I don't think they get anything extra at all. Just look at them. He probably doesn't know that they need it."

She sniffed at the air. "There's plenty of cattle-lick round here, Rra, isn't there?"

The smile grew proud. "Naturally. This is cattle-lick headquarters, you might say."

She took his arm and began to walk to her van. She had something to explain to him, and she did this as they walked together. When they reached the van, they stood for a while longer. He nodded from time to time, with the air of one to whom something was becoming clear. Then she drove off and Mr. Seleo returned to his office.

In her van, Mma Ramotswe started to smile. It's infectious, she thought.

CHAPTER FIFTEEN

AN OFFER OF HELP

"ONE WEEK ONLY!" exclaimed Mma Potokwane. "My, my! In one week you will be Mma Grace Radiphuti! Just think of that!"

Mma Potokwane had dropped in on the offices of the No. 1 Ladies' Detective Agency ostensibly to share a cup of tea with her old friend Mma Ramotswe, but in reality with the ulterior motive of asking Mr. J.L.B. Matekoni to fix the orphan farm tractor. This tractor, an ancient grey machine, had been nursed by Mr. J.L.B. Matekoni over the years—all at no cost—and could generally be persuaded to do what was asked of it; now, however, the wheel on one side appeared to be turning at a different speed from its counterpart on the other, resulting in the tractor's refusal to travel in a straight line without vigorous correction by the driver. "Could Mr. J.L.B. Matekoni possibly come out and take a look at it?" Mma Potokwane had asked as Mma Ramotswe came to meet her outside the office.

"I'm sure he can," said Mma Ramotswe. And he would; her soft-hearted husband, she knew, would never turn down a request from the orphan farm.

"I shall bake him a cake," said Mma Potokwane, who knew of

the mechanic's soft spot for the heavy and immensely rich fruit cake for which she was so well known throughout southern Botswana. In her view, it was a fair exchange of the sort that kept the orphan farm running: a whole list of skills of one sort or another could be called upon in return for her cake. This was how the accountant was paid (ten cakes a year); how the painter and decorator was rewarded (three cakes per room); and, in the case of Mr. J.L.B. Matekoni, two large slices of cake for attention to a small mechanical or electrical problem, and a complete cake for each larger or more time-consuming chore.

Mr. J.L.B. Matekoni's services having been booked, Mma Potokwane and Mma Ramotswe had made their way into the office, where Mma Makutsi was sitting at her desk contemplating one of her to-do lists. It was her last day at work before going off on four days' pre-wedding leave, and her filing, accounts, and typing tasks were all up-to-date.

When Mma Potokwane made her remark about only a week being left, Mma Makutsi beamed with pleasure. She and Mma Potokwane did not enjoy the closest of relationships, but this was not a time to be on difficult terms with anybody. Besides, Mma Potokwane had been treating Mma Makutsi with more consideration recently, owing, Mma Ramotswe thought, to the impending change of Mma Makutsi's status. It was nothing to do with Mma Makutsi's origins—Mma Potokwane was completely indifferent to such matters, but she showed the tendency that many women of her generation had not to take unmarried women completely seriously. *That's what you may think now,* such an attitude implied, *but just wait until you're married—you'll think differently then.* That view was not intended unkindly or cuttingly, but of course there was nothing more annoying for those at whom such condescension was directed, and this went some way to explaining the tension between the orphan-farm matron and Mma Makutsi.

"Yes, it's on Saturday," Mma Makutsi said. "And there is still a lot to do."

Mma Potokwane settled herself into the client's chair. "There is always so much to do when you're getting ready for a wedding," she said. "There's so much that can go wrong—and it usually does."

Mma Ramotswe, who was busy switching on the kettle, pointed out that Mma Makutsi was very well organised. "I don't think anything will go wrong with this wedding," she said reassuringly.

"I hope not," said Mma Potokwane. "But there is always something. There is always something unforeseeable."

Mma Makutsi was listening to this attentively. "Such as, Mma? What unforeseeable things?"

Mma Potokwane smiled. "I cannot answer that," she said. "And that is because unforeseeable things cannot be foreseen. So I do not know what they are."

Mma Makutsi glanced at her list. "What sort of thing, though, Mma? To do with guests? To do with food?"

"Both of these," said Mma Potokwane.

"It will be a very big wedding, this one," interjected Mma Ramotswe. She did not want Mma Makutsi to be unsettled just when she seemed to be getting on top of all the arrangements.

"That is very nice," said Mma Potokwane, in a slightly strained tone. She and her husband had not been invited to the wedding; lines had had to be drawn, and they were on the wrong side. "I like large weddings. It is so kind of the people getting married to invite all their friends—that way nobody feels left out, Mma."

"It is very difficult," said Mma Ramotswe quickly. "Often the couple want to invite everybody, but cannot do so because there simply is not enough room. Everybody understands that, of course."

"I'm sure they do," said Mma Potokwane, in the same rather pinched voice.

Mma Makutsi looked up from her list. "What sort of unforeseeable things, Mma? Can you give me examples?"

"Certainly," said Mma Potokwane. "Guests. How do you know that family members travelling down from wherever will not bring extra relatives with them? Then where do you put these people? You may have arranged for places to stay for everybody on the list, but what about those who are not? That can be a big problem."

Mma Makutsi sat quite still. She had arranged accommodation for forty people from Bobonong—staying with friends of the Radiphuti family, or with distant relatives on the Makutsi side. It had been a major feat of calculation and persuasion, and she did not know what she could do if any more people turned up unannounced, expecting a bed to be found for them for three or four days.

Mma Potokwane noticed the other woman's uncertainty. "Yes," she continued. "There's that problem. And then there's another one. Problems come in threes, I find, Mma. So the next one—problem number two, so to speak—is the cooking of food. You know what I find, Mma, it is this: the people doing the cooking *never* have enough pots. They say they do, but they do not. And right at the last moment they discover that there are not enough pots or, more likely, the pots they have are too small. A pot may be big enough to cook your meat and pap at home, just for a family, but do not imagine that it will be big enough to cook for a couple of hundred people. You need big, catering-size pots for that."

She was now warming to her theme. "And the third problem is the food itself. You may think that you have enough for the feast, and you may be right when it comes to the meat. People usually have enough meat—often rather too much, in fact. But they forget that after their guests have eaten a lot of meat, they need something sweet, and often they have made no arrangements for that. A wedding cake? Yes, but there will only be one small piece of that for each guest—usually not enough. So people find themselves wishing that they had had the foresight to get a supply of ordinary cake for the guests to eat with their tea. And where is this cake? Not there, Mma."

Mma Ramotswe glanced at Mma Makutsi; this was not the way to speak to a nervous bride, she thought. "I'm sure that everything will work out well," she said reassuringly. "And if there are any problems, they will surely just be small ones—nothing to worry about."

Mma Potokwane looked doubtful. "I hope so," she said. "But in my experience it never works out like that. I think it's better to be realistic about these things."

Mma Makutsi picked up her pencil to add something to her list. "You said something about pots, Mma. Where would I be able to get these big, catering-size pots?"

Mma Potokwane examined her fingernails. "Well, we have them at the orphan farm. Each of the house-mothers has a very large pot. I'm sure that we could do something . . ."

Mma Makutsi seized her chance. "Oh, would you, Mma?"

"I'll see what I can do," Mma Potokwane said. "And I wondered if I could help out with cake. There are many people, I believe, who like my cake."

Mma Makutsi made a mental calculation. "You're very kind, Mma," she said. "And I was wondering—I know it's short notice—but I was wondering whether you would care to come to the wedding too? You and your husband, of course."

Mma Potokwane waited a decent interval of time before replying. "Come to the wedding? Well, I hadn't thought of that, but yes, I think that we might be free."

"Well, that's settled, then," said Mma Makutsi.

Mma Potokwane gave Mma Ramotswe a triumphant look. She suspected that her friend thought that she was occasionally a little bit too pushy, but there were times when pushiness was the only way to get what you wanted. Mma Ramotswe needed to learn that, and if she asked in the right way, Mma Potokwane would be prepared to teach her.

The conversation now moved to other topics, including the forthcoming by-election.

"It will be the same result as before," said Mma Potokwane. "It always is. Some will vote for the Government, and others will not. There will be many speeches made, and we all know exactly what will be in these speeches."

Mma Ramotswe laughed. "You never know, Mma. There may be some surprises."

She poured the tea and handed her guest a cup before giving one to Mma Makutsi.

"But there is a big threat in this election," Mma Makutsi said. "One of the candidates . . ."

Mma Ramotswe remembered. "Oh, of course." She turned to Mma Potokwane. "Violet Sephotho is standing. Do you know her, Mma?"

Mma Potokwane put down her cup so quickly that she spilled half her tea. "Violet Sephotho? That woman?"

Mma Makutsi nodded sadly. "Yes. I knew her at the Botswana Secretarial College, you know. We were contemporaries."

"She is a danger to Botswana," said Mma Potokwane. "If she gets anywhere near power, then we are—"

"Finished," supplied Mma Makutsi.

Mma Potokwane asked which constituency Violet was standing in, and was told that it was the constituency next to her own. She groaned. "That is a big tragedy," she said. "We must stop her."

Mma Makutsi needed no persuading. "Yes, we must. I was saying the same thing to Patricia at the clothing shop a few days ago." She frowned. "But how do you stop a political candidate from standing? We are a democracy. You cannot stop somebody from standing for election."

"You can stop them winning," suggested Mma Ramotswe. "You can tell people about them and hope that they'll make the right decision."

"Too late for that," said Mma Potokwane. "No, something else is needed." She looked thoughtful. "Do you think that she wants to get into parliament because she thinks she would like the work?"

Mma Makutsi snorted. "Violet, work? She is not one of these people who are made for work," she said. "She did no work at the Botswana Secretarial College and she hasn't done any since. No, it is not the work."

"Then what is it?" asked Mma Potokwane.

Mma Makutsi said that she thought it was the power, and possibly the glamour, that had attracted Violet to politics.

"It's not all power and glamour, though, is it?" said Mma Potokwane. "It's a lot of hard work—answering letters from constituents, dealing with complaints and so on. That's not the sort of thing that Violet likes, I think."

"I knew a politician once," said Mma Ramotswe. "He used to complain about having to deal with letters from members of the public. He said they expected him to solve all their problems, even to arrange rainfall during a dry spell. It very nearly drove him mad, he said."

Mma Potokwane picked up her cup again and took a sip of tea. "It would be interesting," she mused, "to see what would happen if Violet were to receive a lot of letters *before* the election—letters from her future constituents asking her to deal with all their problems." She paused, watching the effect of her words on the others. "Not small problems—big, difficult problems."

A smile began to cross Mma Makutsi's face. "You don't happen to know people in her constituency, do you, Mma Potokwane?"

Mma Potokwane took a further sip of tea. "I might," she said. "Let me think about it."

She thought for only a few moments.

"It can be done," she said. "I think that we'll be able to persuade Violet that being a politician is no fun."

THAT NIGHT, Mma Ramotswe had a vivid dream. She was with Mma Potokwane and they were searching for cooking pots in a dark storeroom. Mma Potokwane was singing a strange, rather haunting song, but Mma Ramotswe was having difficulty in making out the words. *There are many pots,* the song began; thereafter the sounds became indistinct. *Potokwane, Pots, Potokwane, Pots*—these words suggested themselves, but she could not be sure. *Poto, Poto, Potokwane.* It was a very strange song.

Mma Potokwane disappeared, as people in dreams so seamlessly do. Now she found herself in a landscape at the same time both familiar and unfamiliar; it was Mochudi, or a place just outside it—a place where there is a great jacaranda tree, its spreading boughs weighed down by age, a tree she knew well from her childhood. Beneath this tree were two chairs, traditional Botswana chairs made of hardwood trunks, decorations—animals and people—carved into the wood; not far away, a traditional house with murals of brown and blue daub, the work of a grandmother, now sitting on a stool by the front door. It was the Botswana of the past, even if it still survived here and there in places where the modern world had now come barging in and destroyed it; and her father was somewhere nearby, she thought; she heard his voice and knew that he was with her. *Our country, Precious,* he said to her. *Our Botswana.*

She looked for him, but could not see him, because she knew, even in the dream, that he was dead. Sometimes people in our dreams are dead but not quite dead, yet still talk to us. *Late people can be loved too.* Yes, of course they can, she thought; and the dream dissolved, faded, and she saw not the landscape of Mochudi but the ceiling above her in the house on Zebra Drive and the first rays of the sun through the window.

She turned in her bed—she had been lying on her right arm and it felt numb, as if it belonged to somebody else who had carelessly left it in her bed. She noticed that she was alone in bed, that Mr. J.L.B. Matekoni, who usually got up after she did, was not in his accustomed position. She sat up and looked about her, half expecting to see him standing in the room somewhere—by the wardrobe, perhaps, dressing himself in his daily khakis—but there was no sign of him.

Mma Ramotswe felt a twinge of alarm. He had been in the bed, had he not, when she drifted off to sleep the previous night? He had. There were, she assumed, marriages where wives did not notice whether or not their husband was in bed with them, but her marriage was not like that. She had said goodnight to Mr. J.L.B. Matekoni before going to sleep—she did that every night, and she would have noticed if she had said goodnight to an empty bed or to a pillow on which no head was resting.

She put on her dressing gown and made her way out of the bedroom into the corridor outside. The children's doors were closed—they would still be asleep, as she always awoke well before they did. The bathroom? She put her head round the door: he was not there.

She went into the kitchen and switched on the kettle. Every so often, when some car needed to be fixed urgently, Mr. J.L.B. Matekoni had to make an unusually early start at the garage. When this happened, though, he usually told her first and she would get up early herself to make his breakfast before he left. Had he said something about this last night and had she forgotten about it? She did not think so.

She looked out of the window. The seasons had changed, but in this period, when the memory of winter was still alive, there were times when the morning air still had a nip in it, and this was one such. A wisp of mist, just detectable, hung over the tree-tops; it would not last, she knew, but seeing it made her want to go outside, to stand under those trees and look up at the sky through their lattice-work of leaves. Mr. J.L.B. Matekoni must have slipped away to the garage and forgotten to tell her; she would make him a large bacon sandwich and take it to him when she herself went into work in an hour or so.

A steaming mug of red bush tea in her hand, she went outside. The doves who had taken up residence in her large acacia were preening themselves on their bough—to all intents and purposes a contented married couple preparing for an ordinary day of whatever work the world had in mind for doves. She smiled at them; they looked down at her for a second or two, fluffing up their neck feathers, and then returned to their task of grooming. She turned the corner of the house.

Then she saw it. In the place where she had parked her blue van the previous evening was her old van. She stood quite still, closing her eyes and then reopening them, fully expecting the hallucination to have corrected itself. But it did not; it was there, as real and substantial as the house, as the garden about it, as the ground upon which she, and the van itself, stood.

She stepped forward, half stumbling in her confusion. As she did so, Mr. J.L.B. Matekoni and Charlie came round the corner of the house. Both were beaming with pleasure, seemingly delighting in the surprise they had created.

Her hand rose to her mouth. "What is this . . . ?"

"It's what you wanted, I think," said Mr. J.L.B. Matekoni. "Or it's what Charlie told me you wanted."

"That's right, Boss," said Charlie.

"So I decided that there was no point in trying to make you love that blue van," Mr. J.L.B. Matekoni went on. "You cannot make somebody love something. They must have love in their heart first."

"That's right, Boss," repeated Charlie.

Mma Ramotswe walked up to the van and opened the driver's door.

"He made a very good job of the restoration," said Mr. J.L.B. Matekoni. "I thought it would be impossible, but it just goes to show that you can do these things if you really set out to. Charlie and I had a really good look at it. It's a very nice job."

"And the blue van?" asked Mma Ramotswe. "What about that?"

"We need a new vehicle for the garage," said Mr. J.L.B. Matekoni. "We can use it for there—if you're happy enough with that. We can sort out the money."

"It is not the money," said Mma Ramotswe. "It has never been the money. No, I am very happy indeed."

She lowered herself into the driver's seat, caressing the steering wheel as she did so. Then she bent forward and kissed the wheel, as tenderly as one might kiss a much-loved child.

"Thank you," she said. "I am very happy now."

"Then I am happy as well," said Mr. J.L.B. Matekoni.

"And me too," said Charlie.

Mma Ramotswe got out of the van. "Have you had breakfast yet, Charlie?" she asked.

He shook his head. "Not yet, Mma. I will have a piece of bread when I get into work."

She shook her head. "No, you will not. You come in right now and I shall make you a couple of eggs and some bacon."

"Oh, Mma," said Charlie. "That sounds very good."

The two of them went inside to watch Mma Ramotswe cooking breakfast. Charlie ate enthusiastically and was served a further two eggs after his initial helping. Then Mma Ramotswe went off to wake the children and begin her day in earnest, starting with the drive to the agency in her tiny white van, just as she had always done in the past, year in and year out, and just as she had never really lost hope of doing once more. She cried a little, out of sheer joy, and stopped for a minute or two at the corner of Zebra Drive to compose herself, so that tears should not interfere with her driving, with her triumphal journey, her proud return.

CHAPTER SIXTEEN

THE MOTHER OF MPHO

WITH MMA MAKUTSI out of the office now, on leave for the final preparations for her wedding, Mma Ramotswe had no excuse for putting off that which she knew she had to do. It was not that Mma Makutsi made it impossible for her to get on with her work; it was really just that if she and her assistant were in the office together, then there always seemed to be something to talk about, some office chore that could be tackled together, or a letter that needed to be dictated.

She thought about dictation. Mma Makutsi was, of course, proud of her skills in this respect, having learned shorthand at the Botswana Secretarial College, where her average speed was one hundred and twenty-eight words per minute.

"I cannot speak at that rate," Mma Ramotswe had said when Mma Makutsi revealed this fact to her. "One hundred and twenty-eight words per minute is very fast, Mma. I am not sure if I can even think at that speed."

Mma Makutsi laughed—the relaxed laugh of one who knows that her secretarial skills are beyond question. "It's true, Mma, that most people cannot write shorthand at even one hundred words per minute. Take Violet Sephotho, for example: she managed forty-two words per minute, and probably couldn't even do that these days. Forty-two words, Mma! It would take all day to write one letter at that rate." She paused; there are some remarks, like some temptations, that simply cannot be resisted—at least by those of us who are made of ordinary human stuff. "Of course, Violet was always much faster in some other matters . . ."

Mma Ramotswe smiled. "I see," she said. "Well, there we are. There are all sorts of people, aren't there?"

It was not a remark with which one could disagree, but Mma Makutsi felt that it did not *convey* very much. Of course there were all sorts of people—surely that went without saying. If there were not all sorts of people then life would be remarkably dull, and indeed she felt that she and Mma Ramotswe would be out of a job. But she did not wish to say anything further about Violet Sephotho: her point had been made, and it was clear enough.

"Typing speed is important too," Mma Makutsi had continued. "I have been known to type at just under one hundred words per minute, Mma. There are some typists who are quicker than that, but I have not met one yet—personally, that is. I have read about these people, but have not met them."

"They will type many pages, those people," said Mma Ramotswe.

"I think so, Mma."

That sort of conversation could go on for hours, and sometimes did. That meant tasks which had been put off would remain undone, and that was exactly what had happened with the Moeti case. Mma Ramotswe knew what she had to do: she had to make a journey out to Mr. Moeti's place and speak to Mpho's mother. This woman, she felt, somehow held the key to what had happened. She was now inclined to discount Mpho's confession, but she would still have to raise with his mother the possibility that the boy was responsible for the attack. She was not looking forward to this, as no mother likes to hear of the delinquency of her son, especially when, as Mma Ramotswe imagined would be the case here, the son was one of the few things she had in this world. People lived for their children, and she could imagine how difficult must be the realisation that your child has done something terrible. What would you do if you discovered that a member of your family—a husband or a son, perhaps—was wanted by the police? Would you have to give him up? Surely no mother would do that.

Her mind wandered. What if she were to discover that Mr. J.L.B. Matekoni were a car thief—that all those cars sitting around the garage were in fact stolen? But that was something she found it impossible to contemplate: Mr. J.L.B. Matekoni was incapable of doing anything underhand or unkind, and if anybody were ever to accuse him of such a thing, she would simply not believe it. And that, she thought, might be how Mpho's mother would react. She remembered now how she had looked when she first met her at Mr. Moeti's house. She looked guilty, and Mma Ramotswe had thought that she might well have been responsible for the attack on the cattle. Now, of course, that guilt made sense: a mother who knows that her son has something to answer for will of course look guilty.

She decided that she would go out to the Moeti farm in the late afternoon. She wanted to speak to Mpho's mother without Mr. Moeti himself being present, and she felt that her best chance of doing that would be when she had finished her work for the day. A domestic helper might return later on to make dinner, serve it, and then wash up, but round about five or six she would probably be allowed to be in her own quarters. She would go there, talk to the woman, and then go to Mr. Moeti and speak to him. She was not yet sure what she would say; there were still matters needing to be resolved, and what she said to him would be dependent on how these worked out.

The trip itself was an unalloyed pleasure. The white van was running quietly and contentedly; the terrible knocking sound was nowhere to be heard, the brakes were responsive and silent, and the suspension was comfortable and evenly balanced. That could change, of course, and the van could resume its list to starboard, but that would be a minor irritation and one that traditionally built people were well accustomed to. The old van, of course, was slower than the new one, but that did not bother Mma Ramotswe in the slightest; she was not the sort of detective—or person, indeed—who needed to get anywhere fast. In her experience, the places one set off for were usually still there no matter when one arrived; it would be different, naturally enough, if towns, villages, houses *moved*—then one might have a real reason to hurry—but they did not. Nor did people themselves move very much, in Mma Ramotswe's experience; she remembered how in Mochudi, in what people fondly called the old days, there were people who could be seen standing or sitting in one place for days on end. If one wanted to see a certain man—an expert in goats—then it was well known that he could be found sitting under a particular tree, and that was where advice on goats could always be obtained. Her father told her that this man had once been accused of stock theft by somebody from a neighbouring village. The police at Mochudi had listened to the complaint but had dismissed it out of hand—and quite rightly too. They had explained that the man in question never went anywhere, as everybody knew very well, and that it was quite out of the question that he could have participated in a stock theft elsewhere. "That shows, Precious," Obed Ramotswe had said, "that if you do one thing all the time, then people will know that is what you do."

The old days: people sometimes laughed at those who talked about the old days, but Mma Ramotswe was not one of them. She knew that all of us, even the youngest, had some old days to remember. Children of ten remember how it was when they were five, just as men or women of fifty remember the way things were when they were twenty; and if those distant pasts are coated with sweetness and longing, then that might be because people indeed felt happier then. She did not think that people now were any *worse* than they used to be, but it was very clear to her that they had less time. In the old days Botswana people were rarely in a rush to get somewhere else—why should they be? Nowadays, people were always thinking of getting somewhere—they travelled around far more, rushing from here to there and then back again. She would never let her life go that way; she would always take the time to drink tea, to look at the sky, and to talk. What else was there to do? Make money? Why? Did money bring any greater happiness than that furnished by a well-made cup of red bush tea and a moment or two with a good friend? She thought not.

I'M SORRY, Mmampho. You never told me your name."

Mma Ramotswe felt that it was her fault. People ignored domestic helpers—presences in the background—and rarely asked their names. She usually did, but had forgotten to do so when she first met this woman; addressing her as *Mother of Mpho* was perfectly polite in such circumstances, of course, but using her real name would be even better.

The courtesy had its effect. "I am Pelenomi, Mma. Thank you."

Mma Ramotswe held out her hands in greeting. She was pleased that she had found the woman at home, as she had hoped to do, and that Mpho did not appear to be there.

"Your little boy?" she asked. "Is he looking after the cattle?"

Pelenomi nodded. "He must count them each night before it gets dark. Then he comes home for his food."

"He has a busy day," said Mma Ramotswe. "School, and then the cattle."

"Yes. He is a good boy, Mma. He works hard." She looked at her visitor. "You have children yourself, Mma?"

Mma Ramotswe explained about the fostering of Puso and Motholeli. "I am their mother now," she said. "Their own mother is late." She paused. "And I have a late baby, Mma. It is a long time ago now."

"But it is never long ago when that happens," said Pelenomi. "I have a late child too, Mma. Mpho had a sister. She was never well. God took her back."

There was a silence—a moment of shared loss. Then Pelenomi asked why Mma Ramotswe had come to see her. "It is something to do with that cattle business?" she asked.

Mma Ramotswe nodded. "It is very difficult, Mma. I am not sure how to talk to you about this."

They were standing outside the entrance to her single-roomed servants' quarters—not much more than a whitewashed shack. Pelenomi now invited Mma Ramotswe inside and sat down—with the natural grace of one accustomed to sitting on the floor. Mma Ramotswe lowered herself to the ground. One should not forget how to sit on the floor, she thought—never, no matter what happened in one's life, no matter where one's life journey took one. A president, she believed, should be able to sit on the floor with as much ease as the humblest herdsman.

"What have you found, Mma?" asked Pelenomi.

"I was at the school, Mma."

Pelenomi stiffened. "At the school? Why?"

"I wanted to speak to Mpho. I didn't want adults to be around him when we spoke. I'm sorry, Mma, I didn't ask your permission—I hope you don't mind. I thought he was a witness, you see."

"He did not see anything. He is just a boy."

Mma Ramotswe said nothing for a moment. Then she said, "He told me that he did it, Mma."

There was no mistaking Pelenomi's surprise. "Mpho told you that, Mma? Oh, that is just a child speaking, Mma. A child says the first thing that comes into his mind. You should not listen to a child. My son did not do anything, Mma. Nothing."

Her voice had risen towards the end of this, as her indignation grew. It was as Mma Ramotswe had imagined—the loyal mother refusing to accept that her son could have done something like that. But what was said next was less than expected.

"No, it is not my son, Mma. It is . . . it is another person altogether." She paused. "I know who it is, Mma. I know."

Mma Ramotswe watched her carefully. This woman was not lying.

"Who then, Mma? Mr. Fortitude Seleo?"

Pelenomi's lip curled. "Not that man. He could not do a thing like that. He is too busy walking around smiling at people."

There was bitterness in this last remark.

"That is better than scowling at them, I think, Mma. But that is neither here nor there. If it is not Seleo, then who is it?"

"It is another man altogether. I cannot name him, Mma. I'm sorry."

"But why did Mpho say that it was him? I saw his face when he told me, Mma. I could tell that he was very upset. A child does not make these things up."

The answer came quickly. "Because he thought it was me, Mma. He thought that his mother had done it. He was frightened for his mother. That is why he told you it was him. A child does not want his mother to go to prison."

"Why did he think it was you?"

"Because he saw something. And I told him. I had to tell him something."

"What did he see?"

Pelenomi was now becoming flustered, and was clearly regretting allowing herself to be pushed into a corner by Mma Ramotswe's questions. "There are some things that children see . . ."

"What did he see, Mma?"

"He saw some blood. He saw a handkerchief with blood on it."

A small insect moved slowly across the floor, a spider perhaps, making Mma Ramotswe move her legs slightly. Pelenomi watched the movement.

"I keep this house clean, Mma," she muttered.

"I'm sure you do. There are ants everywhere. It is not your fault. But what about this handkerchief, Mma?"

The misery came through Pelenomi's voice. "It was the handkerchief of the man who had done that thing to the cattle. He was in this house after he had done it. Mpho was asleep—he never wakes up. He saw the cloth in the morning."

"And he thought it was yours?"

Pelenomi nodded. "I told him it was mine. I told him that Moeti had done some bad thing to me and that I had taken my revenge on his cattle. That is why he lied to protect me."

Unless, thought Mma Ramotswe, *you are lying to protect him.*

There was a knock on the door, a voice muttering *Ko! Ko!*

Pelenomi looked up in alarm and began to scramble to her feet. *Moeti?* wondered Mma Ramotswe. The door opened before she could reach it and a man stepped into the room. He stood for a moment, confused by the unexpected presence. It was not Moeti. Oreeditse Modise, the teacher at the school.

He'd come in with the confidence of one entering the house of his lover. And that, Mma Ramotswe decided at that moment, was exactly what he was. She did not have to think about it: the dwarf was the lover of Mpho's mother. And more than that: he was the man who had attacked the cattle. Of course he was; why else had he and his secretary exclaimed their outrage over the incident with such forcefulness? That had been an act: he was the perpetrator, and the secretary must somehow have come into that information. But why had he done it? Pelenomi had given a clue to that in saying that she had made up a story about her being a victim of Moeti. Well, she had not made it up; she was. And Modise had avenged her in the way they knew would cause maximum distress to Moeti.

They looked at each other wordlessly. Then Mma Ramotswe rose to her feet and dusted off her skirt. "I mustn't stay, Mma," she said. "Now that you have another visitor."

The teacher was staring at her. She met his gaze.

"I have been looking into this cattle problem," Mma Ramotswe said quietly. "Now I must go. But there are a few questions I would like an answer to. Please think carefully before you give me your reply."

Pelenomi and Modise exchanged glances. Then Modise nodded. "What are these questions, Mma?"

"My questions," began Mma Ramotswe, "are these ones, Rra. Would I be right in thinking that this very bad thing that has happened here will not happen again? Would I be right in thinking that if I were to tell Moeti that everything is over, that not one more of his cattle will suffer, then there would be no more of this sort of thing happening? Would I be right in thinking that the person who did this would realise that I could go to the police if I wanted to and insist that they sorted it all out? Would that person—whoever he might be—also understand that there is no excuse for settling one wrong with another?"

There was a further exchange of glances between Modise and

Pelenomi. Then he spoke: "I think you would be right, Mma. I am sure of it."

"Good," said Mma Ramotswe. "Then that is the end of that, I think."

SHE LEFT THE VAN where it was and walked over to the Moeti farmhouse. She found him in his living room, listening to the Radio Botswana news. He greeted her cheerfully and offered her a cold beer, which she declined.

"I hoped that you might have celebrated with me, Mma Ramotswe," he said. "But I can drink your beer too! A bigger celebration for me."

She was puzzled. "Celebrating, Rra?"

"Yes. Celebrating your solving the issue of my poor cattle." He reached for a beer from a tray on his side table. "Here goes, Mma Ramotswe. Here's to the top detective who sorts everything out one hundred per cent. Here's to you!"

"You are happy, Rra?" she said lamely.

"Happy? Yes, of course I am. Seleo came to see me. Not to complain this time but to tell me that he had arranged for the fencing work to start on Tuesday. So no more trespassing by his cattle. But he did something else—to make up for all my inconvenience. He has given me six months' supply of cattle-lick for my cattle."

Mma Ramotswe was at a loss as to what to say.

"I think what happened was that you must have put the fear of God into him, Mma. Once he realised that the country's top detective was on to him, he must have caved in and decided to apologise. And there's another thing, Mma. He gave me the cash value of the cattle he did that terrible thing to. A good price. So I am happy now to say that it is all over. We can be good neighbours again. That is the Botswana way, and that is what I want."

Mma Ramotswe looked up at the ceiling. She had no idea what to make of this, but she knew that whichever way one looked at it, this was an entirely satisfactory outcome. She might not be completely certain who carried out the attack on the cattle, but the issue was well and truly put to bed. It was not Mpho, she thought; and although until a few moments ago she had thought it was the teacher, that conclusion had now been called into question. Pelenomi had effectively blamed Modise, but if he had done it, why had Seleo acted as he had? She had advised him to make some sort of friendly approach to Moeti and to give him a gift of cattle-lick. He had then gone further than that—much further—and had more or less acknowledged his guilt by compensating his neighbour for the loss of his cattle. Why would he do that? Unless, of course, he was trying to protect the real culprit—the teacher? But what possible reason could he have to do that?

She continued to stare up at the ceiling. Perhaps everybody is lying, she thought. And as she thought this, she remembered a passage from Clovis Andersen. *There are some cases where everybody tells lies,* he wrote. *In these cases you will never know the truth. The more you try to find out what happened, the more lies you uncover. My advice is: do not lose sleep over such matters. Move on, ladies and gentlemen: move on.*

She continued to think about it as she drove home. She was now inclined to acquit Mr. Seleo, who was exactly as the security guard had described him. He was a good man who had decided to see whether a generous approach to his neighbour would heal their rift. And it had. No, it was not him. It was the teacher, then—the jealous lover who resented the way Mr. Moeti had treated the woman he loved. Or—and she kept coming back to this possibility—it really had been Mpho, that poor little boy who was desperate for attention and filled with anger at the man who had harmed his mother in some unspoken way. And the mother had then so engineered things that Mma Ramotswe would think it was the teacher, in order to cover for her son . . . or for herself.

These questions occupied her mind all the way back to Gaborone. She was sure that it was one of the three: Mpho, his mother, or the teacher. The mother had been genuinely surprised at Mpho's confession, and that pointed to his innocence. If it was not the boy, then, it was the mother, or the teacher. Of the two, she favoured the teacher as the culprit; the attack itself did not seem to be the work of a woman. She was not sure why she felt that; she just did. A woman knows what another woman will do, she thought.

But then, as she reached the edge of the city, she suddenly smiled and said to herself: "Does it really matter? The milk is spilled. It will not be spilled again." There would be no further attacks—that was clear, and the damage had been set right by one who was not responsible for it. All that was lacking was the punishment of the one responsible. But punishment often did not do what we wanted it to do. If the teacher were to be denounced, he could lose his job and then Mpho and his mother could lose the man who was their one chance of something better. There was no reason for her to bring that about.

This thought of milk brought tea to her mind. She needed tea—a large cup of it—and that was what she would make when she returned home to Zebra Drive. She would say to Mr. J.L.B. Matekoni: "A dreadfully difficult case, Rra, all sorted out now. But don't ask me to explain how it worked out, Rra. There are some things that are just too hard to explain, and I think that this is one of them."

Perhaps she would say that. Perhaps. But she was not sure whether she would *think* that, as she was now reaching a firmer conclusion. The teacher did it. It *was* him. Yes, definitely. Or perhaps . . .

CHAPTER SEVENTEEN

SHE CRIED FOR JOY

WHEN HE READ ALOUD the wedding invitation Mr. J.L.B. Matekoni had said, "At long last the elder Mr. Radiphuti and the late Mrs. Radiphuti have pleasure in inviting you to the wedding of their beloved Phuti Edgar Radiphuti, to Grace Makutsi, Dip. Sec. RSVP."

He had corrected himself immediately. "It doesn't actually say *at long last,* Mma Ramotswe. That was me. It just says *The elder Mr. Radiphuti,* and so on."

Mma Ramotswe smiled. "I see that the invitation is also from the late mother," she said. "I'm not sure whether that wording is quite right, but that does not matter. The important thing is, as you say, that at long last those two are getting married." She also had some doubt about putting RSVP so close to Dip. Sec. as some people—perhaps some of the older country guests—might interpret RSVP as a qualification and wonder what it was.

These were little things, though, as Mma Ramotswe pointed out. What counted was that on that particular Saturday, Mma Makutsi was to become Mrs. Phuti Radiphuti; that the weather was behaving itself, with no unexpected storm to disrupt proceedings; that the bus bringing the Makutsi guests down from Bobonong had made the journey with no greater disaster than a flat tyre just outside Mahalapye; and that all the arrangements for the wedding feast had gone as smoothly as could possibly be hoped for.

This last achievement was partly to the credit of Mma Potokwane, who had interpreted Mma Makutsi's acceptance of help with the pots and with cake as a green light to take over control of all aspects of the feast. Nobody had objected to this, not even Mma Makutsi, who, although she had in the past been irritated by Mma Potokwane's controlling tendencies, found them a great reassurance now.

"She is like a hurricane," Mma Makutsi whispered to Mma Ramotswe on Friday morning when Mma Ramotswe phoned her to check that all was well. "She is in the next room right now, and there is a lot of banging of pots and some big thumping sounds that I cannot make out."

"Cakes," suggested Mma Ramotswe. "That is the sound of her cakes being taken out of their tins."

"Maybe, Mma. Now I think they are chopping something, but I do not know what it is."

"She will make sure that everything is all right," said Mma Ramotswe. "I remember what she did at my own wedding. She got all the house-mothers at the orphan farm to do the cooking. She was like a general telling the Botswana Defence Force what to do. March this way, march that way—that sort of thing."

"I don't think she will let anything go wrong," said Mma Makutsi, not without relief.

In this, she proved to be right. With the same efficiency and determination with which she organised the affairs of the orphan farm, Mma Potokwane ensured that everything was cooked and ready well before the guests began to file into the church where the ceremony was to be held. So while the guests waited in their pews, craning their necks to look at and admire the fine outfits that everybody had donned for the occasion—the bright traditional print dresses of the women, the smartly pressed blue suits of the men, the colourful voile frocks of the little girls—back in the grounds of the Radiphuti house the tables along the sides of the tent were already stacked with pots of meat, with large bowls of gravy, with pumpkin and peas, with every sort of dish that anybody present might wish for. Mma Potokwane had left nothing to chance, and had been delighted to discover the generosity of the catering budget that the Radiphuti family had made available. If anybody came to the feast hungry or undernourished, she felt, then they would not go away in that state. Belts could be loosened if necessary, collars unbuttoned; it would be a memorable feast.

Mma Ramotswe had been allocated a seat in the front row, alongside Mr. J.L.B. Matekoni. Puso and Motholeli were in the row immediately behind them, seated beside two other children from Bobonong, with whom they had formed those instant friendships that children seem to manage so effortlessly. A little further behind, Charlie and Fanwell, both wearing shiny suits and bright ties, studied their hymn sheets conscientiously. When the time came to sing, as the bride entered on the arm of her uncle, the two young men proved to be enthusiastic singers, even if in different keys from each other.

As Mma Makutsi entered the church, a ripple of applause broke out at the back and spread through the congregation. Children waved, and some of the women ululated—a traditional sign of pleasure, pride, and congratulation. Mma Makutsi's eyes were moist behind her large glasses; it had been so long a journey for her, and now she was at its culmination, in the presence of her family and those whom she loved. She saw their faces—the aunt who had helped her financially, in every small way that she could, who had paid for that first bus journey that she made to Gaborone all those years ago; the cousins who had written to her regularly and had so generously congratulated her on each small triumph; and there, halfway down the church, in an aisle seat and turned to face her as she took those few steps to the altar, was the retired Principal of the Botswana Secretarial College, smiling with pride at her own, indirect role in bringing about the career that had led to all this.

Mma Ramotswe's eyes, and the eyes of every woman present, were on the dress. It was magnificent: a floor-length creation of ivory satin, with large puffed sleeves and a sash round the waist. At the back, this sash was tied in a giant bow, like the wings of a butterfly. The bodice was trimmed with white lace, and around her neck Mma Makutsi wore a delicate gold chain with a pendant cross, a gift from Phuti Radiphuti, the groom who now awaited her at the altar.

There would be many speeches in the wedding tent later on. Now, as Phuti Radiphuti stepped forward to take his bride from the uncle, and as the congregation finished the opening hymn, the minister cleared his throat.

"Dearly beloved," he began, "we are gathered here in this place to bring together in marriage two people, our brother and our sister, Phuti and Grace. They are being married here because they love one another and they declare that love now before you, this congregation, and before all Botswana. If there is any person who knows of any reason why these two people cannot be joined together in marriage by the laws of this country, then that person must now speak."

There was silence. Charlie glanced at Fanwell, and winked.

The minister continued, "And so I shall now ask them to exchange their vows. Phuti, please take Grace's hand. That is right. Now then . . ."

The marriage was solemnised. Mma Ramotswe watched, and from her position so close to the front heard every word of the vows.

She had so many memories: of her first meeting with Mma Makutsi, who had presented herself for interview with such confidence and determination; of her initial difficulties in coming to terms with her new assistant's rather prickly behaviour; of her growing appreciation for her many fine qualities; of her pleasure when eventually she had found Phuti Radiphuti and her delight in their engagement. Mma Makutsi had been fortunate in finding Phuti, but fortune had also smiled on Mma Ramotswe, who now glanced tenderly at Mr. J.L.B. Matekoni at her side. He noticed her glance, and touched the sleeve of her dress lightly, a small gesture that conveyed so much.

Mma Ramotswe cried, privately and unseen. She, the only begetter of the No. 1 Ladies' Detective Agency, cried. She cried for joy.

AFTERWARDS, they left the church and went to the wedding tent at the Radiphuti house. Now the sound of voices rose, and there were children and dogs, and even one or two interested birds circling overhead. The uncle with the broken nose—the greedy one from Bobonong—made the main speech on Mma Makutsi's side. Mma Ramotswe tried to follow what he had to say, but it seemed to her that it was hopelessly confused—some story of a cow that had run off to another field but who never forgot the cows back in the first field. It was a message of some sort, she assumed, but nobody seemed to be very interested in it. It was not very tactful, she thought, to use cow metaphors when one was talking about a bride, but Mma Makutsi herself did not seem to mind, and clapped as loudly as everybody else did when the uncle eventually sat down.

Mma Makutsi moved from table to table, from chair to chair, talking to the guests, accepting good wishes, showing her bouquet of flowers to the children, and doing her duty as hostess, as the new Mma Radiphuti. When she reached Mma Ramotswe's table, at first she did not say anything, but leaned forward and embraced the woman who had given her her one great chance in life, who had been such a good friend to her.

Then she spoke. "I am still going to be coming into the No. 1 Ladies' Detective Agency, Mma," she said. "This will not change things. I shall still be working."

"I will be waiting for you," said Mma Ramotswe. "After your honeymoon, of course."

She looked at the bride. She saw the shoes.

"The shoes you gave me, Mma," Mma Makutsi said. "They are very beautiful."

Mma Ramotswe smiled. "Charlie did his best, didn't he?"

Mma Makutsi inclined her head graciously. "He did. It was very good of him to try."

They both laughed. Charlie had tried to fix the original pair of broken shoes, and had not done too bad a job. He had done it discreetly, unasked, taking the shoes from a cupboard in the office and returning them a couple of days later. Mma Makutsi had been touched by this, even if his repair had in the end been inadequate. It was a peace offering, and she accepted it, for her part apologising for jumping to unwarranted conclusions in the affair of the twins. And that brought forth an apology from him. "You are not a warthog," he said. "I am very sorry, Mma, for saying that."

Mma Ramotswe had then slipped out and bought a new pair of shoes for Mma Makutsi—ones that she thought would be suitable for the wedding. These had proved perfect, and Mma Makutsi had shown them to Phuti Radiphuti at the same time as she confessed to the destruction of their predecessors. He had not minded in the least. "The important thing is that you didn't hurt your ankle," he said. "That is what counts."

THERE WERE MANY SPEECHES, mostly by relatives on either side. Weddings and speeches went together, and the guests listened patiently, knowing that there would be more food later on. That food kept the guests busy for the best part of two hours. Then there was music, provided by the Big Time Kalahari Jazz Band. This led to dancing, with Mma Makutsi and Phuti Radiphuti taking to the floor to general applause and whistles. The dance lessons they had both taken all that time ago came in useful, and Phuti, who had not been a particularly good dancer to begin with, proved competent enough now, even with his artificial foot. After that first dance, Mma Makutsi danced with Mr. J.L.B. Matekoni, and Mma Ramotswe was invited to dance with the uncle with the broken nose. She put on a brave face over this, managing to control her winces as the uncle trod heavily on her toes and pushed her clumsily about the floor of the tent. It was a great relief to her when the band stopped and she was able to make her way back to her chair.

Eventually it was time to leave, and Mma Ramotswe and Mr. J.L.B. Matekoni drove home in the white van, with Mma Ramotswe at the wheel. It was early evening now, and Mr. J.L.B. Matekoni, who was feeling tired, went off to have his somewhat delayed Saturday afternoon nap. After the feast there would be no question of dinner, so she had no cooking to do. The children had gone to a friend's house for the night; Mma Ramotswe was alone.

She went out into the garden. The sun had set, but there was still a faint glow in the west, above the Kalahari—enough to provide that half-light that makes everything seem so rounded, so perfect. She stood in her garden and looked about her. Against the gradually darkening sky, the branches of the trees traced a pattern of twigs and leaves—a pattern of such intricacy and delicacy that those standing below might look up and wonder why the world can be so beautiful and yet break the heart.

She stood still for a while, thinking about marriage. A wedding was a strange ceremony, she thought, with all those formal words, those solemn vows made by one to another; whereas the real question that should be put to the two people involved was a very simple one. *Are you happy with each other?* was the only question that should be asked; to which they both should reply, preferably in unison, *Yes.* Simple questions—and simple answers—were what we needed in life. That was what Mma Ramotswe believed. Yes.

She went back into the house, as night had come over the town, the sky suddenly going from deep blue into black—and stars had appeared over Africa. She gave one last glance towards the horizon, to check whether the Southern Cross was where it should be. It was.

africa
africa africa
africa africa africa
africa africa
africa

ABOUT THE AUTHOR

Alexander McCall Smith is the author of the No. 1 Ladies' Detective Agency series, the Isabel Dalhousie series, the Portuguese Irregular Verbs series, and the 44 Scotland Street series. He is professor emeritus of medical law at the University of Edinburgh and has served on many national and international bodies concerned with bioethics. He was born in what is now known as Zimbabwe and taught law at the University of Botswana. He lives in Scotland.